# ATTACK IN THE DARK

McNeil had turned halfway around when he heard the crackling of bushes and the sound of running feet behind him. Damn! He should have taken the .45—before he could complete the thought the attackers were on him.

There were two of them; both dressed in black, with dark stockings over their heads. They tried to jump him, but McNeil aimed his elbow where he guessed the man's groin would be, and his guess was correct. The attacker let out an ear-splitting scream of agony. Then McNeil swung his fist into the other man's jaw, hurling him into the bushes.

McNeil yelled for help. His eyes roamed around and spotted the fallen briefcase. So did the attacker . . . and he got there first, snatching the briefcase under one arm. Then he drew a small automatic from his pocket and fired twice at point-blank range. One bullet lashed the side of McNeil's face and ear, the other stung his ribs.

He dropped flat on the ground, and the attackers vanished—and with them the secret plans for Operation Endless Voyage.

# THE ULTIMATE WEAPON

## by Edward Grant

PINNACLE BOOKS  •  NEW YORK CITY

This is a work of fiction. All the characters and events portrayed in this book are fictional, and any resemblance to real people or incidents is purely coincidental.

THE ULTIMATE WEAPON

*Copyright © 1976 by Lyle Kenyon Engel*

An original Pinnacle Books edition, published for the first time anywhere.

ISBN: 0-523-00832-5

First printing, March 1976

Cover illustration by Dean Cate

*Printed in the United States of America*

PINNACLE BOOKS, INC.
275 Madison Avenue
New York, N.Y. 10016

# ULTIMATE WEAPON

I

Two hundred miles off the coast of Virginia, the Atlantic Ocean runs deep. The continental shelf has long since dropped off into the depths. Between the ooze on the bottom and the sunlight on the surface lies nearly two miles of black, chill water. Since the oceans began, these waters have been home to the fish of the open sea, nothing else. Men and their ships have sailed across the surface, but never have they entered these depths alive and intact.

But the waters are disturbed now, by the passage of something that is neither fish nor sunken ship. It is a submarine, racing west at a speed and depth that no submarine has ever reached before. Twin propellers drive her through the black waters at the speed of a fast train, while inside her are sixty men, warm and comfortable. Inside her hull they are safe from the blackness, the cold, and the crushing pressure outside. They do not forget what lies outside, waiting to leap on them if they make one mistake, or if their ship has one failure.

But they will not make that mistake. They are experienced submariners, the pick of the United States Navy. And their ship will not fail them.

She is *Devilfish*, and there are no others like her.

Commander John Cheever, U.S.N., leaned back in the glossy leather command chair in *Devilfish*'s control room and watched the master displays in front of him. Normally there was no need for him to be here, since he didn't believe in looking over his crew's shoulders. They all knew their jobs, and the jobs of six or seven of their mates as well. Anyone who wasn't that good would never have been aboard *Devilfish*, the latest—and perhaps the last—word in atomic submarines.

But *Devilfish*'s newness and advanced design meant that she was also breaking a new trail with every mile that she sailed and every maneuver she attempted. And John Cheever had an endlessly searching, endlessly curious, analytical mind, almost as much the mind of a scientist or an engineer as it was the mind of a brilliant young naval officer. He took every possible opportunity to drive *Devilfish* to the limits of her performance, watching for unsuspected weaknesses or unsuspected abilities in his magnificent new ship.

Aboard *Devilfish* there was no book to follow. Aboard *Devilfish* they were writing their own book.

Besides, the master control center was always a fascinating sight. After nearly a year of working out on mock-ups and six months of watching the real thing in action, Cheever still enjoyed it.

It spread around the entire forward end of the control room and rose up to the gray-blue overhead. In the center was a giant holographic tank, with a thin white ribbon unwinding through its blackness—*Devilfish*'s track through the deep. Far below the white line an undulating surface unrolled—the bottom, continuously mapped by *Devilfish*'s sonar. Equally far above the surface of the Atlantic.

Cheever took a closer look at the blackness in the tank. It was on medium-scale setting now, showing a radius of about twenty miles around *Devilfish*. At maximum setting, her active sonar and passive listening gear could paint a complete picture of everything in the ocean within sixty miles. And then the computer array just below the control room could convert it into a complete three-dimensional picture for the holotank.

Within that twenty miles, the display showed nothing that Cheever needed to worry about. Eight miles away on a bearing of 270 was a school of whales; a jagged bump on the bottom suggested a sunken ship. What kind of ship was it, Cheever wondered, and how had it come there? These waters had been swallowing ships and men for centuries. Idly he reached over and jabbed a button on his personal board. That would cause the ship's navigational computer to record the position of the bump on *Devilfish's* track tape so that they could find it easily again. The bottom here was less than 11,000 feet down, well within *Devilfish's* diving range.

In any case, the sea for a good many miles around was clear of anything that might be dangerous to *Devilfish*, or curious about her. This was as good a time and place as any to once more put *Devilfish* through one of the maneuvers that she alone could perform.

Cheever grinned. "Rig diving planes for high-speed maneuvering," he said quietly. Aboard a submarine there was seldom any reason to shout an order. But when there was—Cheever had vivid memories of the few times in his twelve years in submarines that men had been shouting orders. He hoped there would never be such a time aboard *Devilfish*.

The machinist's mate 1/c who was planesman of the watch nodded.

"Aye aye, sir." The planesman's hand reached casually forward to his control panel and flicked a knobby switch. Like all the other men qualified to stand control room watches, he could operate any and all of the switches on his board and all the others blindfolded—or in total darkness.

A faint shudder ran through the ship. The diving planes mounted on the "sail" projecting from the hull

3

above the control room were being rigged in. Normally it was these planes that controlled *Devilfish's* ascents and descents, but for a while they would be unnecessary. In fact, they would even be in danger of being torn off.

Then Cheever gave his next order into the intercom. "Flank speed."

A bell rang and a light went on above the speed telegraph. The engine room was acknowledging the order. A hundred feet astern, the engine room watch would be opening switches and pulling levers, feeding more power from the reactor into the twin propellers.

Those propellers were one of the more unorthodox parts of this unorthodox ship. They were not driven by turbines geared to shafts that ran through the hull— there was no way to seal such openings in *Devilfish's* fiberglass hull against the pressure of three miles of water. So the turbines drove electromagnetic generators, which created a small but powerful magnetic field that reached out to the propeller shafts through the heavy glass of the capsules in which the shafts were mounted. Rotating rapidly, the field transmitted its rotation to the shafts and they passed it to the six-bladed propellers. The glass of the shaft capsules could stand ten miles of water, let alone three, and there was no gearing to break down.

As her propellers began to turn faster, *Devilfish* began to quiver slightly, then tilted even more slightly to port. The chief of the watch gently turned his control wheel, and the tilt straightened out as quickly as it had begun. Cheever kept his eyes on the speed indicator, watching the white needle climb across the green dial.

*Devilfish* had been cruising at forty-five knots—fifty-five miles an hour—on little more than half power. Now the reactor was feeding nearly twice as much power into the propellers and the speed began to increase. Soon it was up to sixty-five knots.

4

Seventy.

Seventy-five.

Eighty.

The vibration began again. *Devilfish* was nearing her limits. The chief of the watch was locking white-knuckled hands on the control wheel. At this speed even the slightest error could throw *Devilfish* disastrously out of control in seconds. And if that happened, she could smash herself against the ocean bottom in minutes.

The needle crept past eighty knots and quivered upward.

Eighty-one.

Eighty-two.

"Well done," said Cheever. The chief of the watch couldn't hold back a sigh of relief. "Hold her there." He turned his head toward the planesman.

"Activate hydroplanes for—" he hesitated for a moment, considering—"twenty-degree up-angle."

"Aye aye, sir." Again a casual reaching out. This time the planesman flicked two switches.

The vibration this time was not slight. *Devilfish* seemed to leap like a startled horse. Then the deck began tilting up, as her bow rose. The inclinometer needle rose with it, sliding upward to ten, fifteen, twenty, twenty-one—

"Ease her off," said Cheever.

The planesman's hands made minute adjustments of the two switches and the upward leap of the bow stopped. Cheever took his eyes off the inclinometer and looked over to the holotank and the depth gauge. The white line in the black tank was angling sharply upward. *Devilfish* was surging up out of the deep ocean at nearly a thousand feet a minute. Cheever's lean face broke into a broad grin. *Devilfish* had done this before, and she would do it again. But he won-

5

dered if he would ever lose his delight and wonder at seeing her do it.

It was really very simple. As Admiral Cappel, *Devilfish's* "father," had put it:

"After we had figured out the hull and powerplant design, we began to realize what we really had here. And that was a submarine that could run through the sea faster than a good many light airplanes can fly! So somebody—I forget who—said, 'If she's as fast as an airplane, why not make her able to maneuver like one?' Nobody could think up any objections, so we went ahead."

Normal submarines dived and rose by taking in or blowing out water from their ballast tanks. It was a slow, delicate process, involving enormous masses of compressed air. It also involved enormous amounts of noise that an alert enemy could hardly miss.

But *Devilfish* was faster than any normal submarine. And she was shaped entirely differently. The normal submarine looks like an elongated football; *Devilfish's* four-inch-thick fiberglass hull had great streamlined wings flaring out to either side of the central cigar, which made her look like a giant manta ray—a devilfish.

But those "wings" gave her other things besides her name. At any speed above ten knots the water flowing past them gave an upward pressure, like the air flowing past the wings of an airplane. At eighty-two knots that pressure became something incredible.

Set in the rear of each wing, port and starboard, was a hinged section that could be adjusted to various angles. When those hinged sections were moved, they changed the flow of water over *Devilfish's* wings. As the water flow changed, so did *Devilfish's* path up or down, with incredible speed and without any noisy blowing of tanks.

Cheever wondered what would happen if he ever ordered maximum rise angle—something like thirty degrees—at flank speed, and held it. *Devilfish* would shoot up out of the depths at well over a thousand feet a minute. If he didn't stop her, she would probably go leaping out of the water like a playful whale and fall back with a splash like nothing seen before on earth. The notion of three thousand tons of submarine putting on a show like that made Cheever smile.

The depth gauge was rising past a thousand feet now. They were back to "shallow" depths, where earlier atomic submarines had reached their limits. *Thresher* had collapsed and died with her one-hundred-twenty-nine men not much deeper than this. *Devilfish* would not collapse until she was more than three miles down.

Five hundred feet now. It was time to slow down and level off. "Two-degree up-angle," said Cheever. "One-third ahead on both." The speed indicator began to drop back across the dial, and the dizzying rise of the depth gauge slowed.

*Devilfish* leveled out three hundred feet below the surface and settled down to an almost leisurely thirty knots. The chief of the watch took a crumpled handkerchief out of his dungarees and mopped his balding forehead. Then he turned to Cheever with a broad grin.

"She did it again, sir."

Cheever nodded silently. He was a quiet man by nature, inclined to keep his thoughts and emotions behind a mask. And at this moment his pride in the magnificent ship and crew under his command was so great that he could not have spoken even if he had felt like it.

Feet sounded above, coming down the ladder from the conning tower. Cheever turned in time to see the grinning face of his executive officer, Lieutenant-Commander Frank Bronson, drop through the hatch.

The sight of the perennially competent, perennially

7

cheerful Bronson helped Cheever to relax again. He rose from the command chair and motioned the officer of the watch to take over.

"Take her up to periscope depth on the ballast tanks, Mr. Orman. Then send a message to ComSubLant that *Devilfish* is proceeding to Norfolk and our ETA at the Virginia Capes is 2130.

"When you've done that, take her down to six hundred feet and keep her there until we're within twenty miles of the hundred-fathom line. Then call me."

"Aye aye, sir."

Bronson had already vanished through the forward door of the control room, the one leading to officers' country and the wardroom. As Cheever headed after him, his mind began working again.

*Devilfish* was on her way back from the last phase of her shakedown cruise, one that had lasted more than twice the normal time. But now, finally, it was over. *Devilfish* was a fully operational submarine; that had proved she could do everything she had been designed to do, and more. Her designers had dreamed a mighty dream when they had put her blueprints on their drawing boards. And her New England builders had worked hard to make that dream a reality.

What was *Devilfish* going to do now? Cheever badly wanted to know. He hoped Admiral Cappel would have the answer when *Devilfish* reached Norfolk.

## 2

Admiral Hugh Cappel shifted uneasily, trying to find a more comfortable position on the metal bucket seat of the helicopter. Finally he gave up. Helicopters and helicopter seats were just not designed for comfort. And there was nothing he was going to be able to do about it, whether he liked it or not. He settled back and looked out the window.

The helicopter was half an hour out of Norfolk Naval Air Station, flying straight out over the Atlantic. They were fifty miles offshore and a thousand feet up. Land was already well out of sight.

Cappel turned his eyes west and shaded them against the sunset. There was not a cloud in the sky, except for a few pink-tinged fringes in the west. The sun was sinking into the sea in a ball of raw orange fire, pouring out more color in a long path across the sea. The darkening ocean below was calm, with only a gentle swell. Getting Johnny Cheever off *Devilfish* would be easy.

Unless they missed the rendezvous. Cappel almost laughed at himself for the thought. Between Cheever and Bronson and *Devilfish*'s computers there wasn't a chance worth worrying about that the submarine would miss the rendezvous. Cappel recognized his concern as just another one of those habits of his going back to the Second World War. Then he had always looked at everything that might go wrong, and so he had survived. He had survived storms and collision, bombs and depthcharges and gunfire, a year in a Japanese prison camp. He had survived them all, to come home in 1945 with the Congressional Medal of Honor and a score of a hundred thousand tons of Japanese shipping sent to the bottom.

Things had been so simple then, and they were so damned complicated now! There were still things to worry about, but they weren't bow-angles on a target or diving below enemy depthcharges any more. As head of the Office of Special Submarine Operations, he was doing things he would never have imagined himself doing that day in 1944 when *Stonefish* took her final dive.

Drawing up budgets. Looking at building plans, not just for docks and machine shops, but for scientific laboratories. Paperwork, paperwork, and more paperwork! Ass-kissing with politicians like Senator Bergen and chair-borne Pentagon types who had never commanded anything but an LSD—Large Steel Desk.

At least he had a fleet under his command for the first time since he had hauled down his flag as ComSubPac. God, that was nearly fifteen years ago! There were two converted yachts, a research vessel, a trio of minisubs, and a batch of small craft. And there was *Devilfish*.

Cappel was almost used to what *Devilfish* was and what she could do by now. But it had taken him a while, and she still had surprises for him. Hell, she still had surprises in her for her own crew, he'd bet! She was a ship full of miracles, and she filled Cappel with pride. Pride in the men who manned her, particularly Johnny Cheever. Pride in the United States Navy that had sent her to sea. And pride in the country whose best brains and hands had brought her from blueprints into a reality. But sometimes she also filled him with a sad realization of how much time had passed since the war, and how old he was getting.

He remembered the Chief of the Boat of Stonefish, a solid Wisconsin German who thought better with his hands than with his balding head. Schwerner had saved Stonefish more than once by knowing damn near everything there was to know about her. But Devilfish? To somebody like old Schwerner, Devilfish would have been like a spaceship from another planet. More power, then, to Johnny Cheever and Frank Bronson and the others who took Devilfish out in "great waters."

A fleck of white on the dark sea caught Cappel's eye. It looked like the feather of a periscope, but it might be—

It wasn't whatever it might have been. The white spread, and became unmistakably the cloud of spray thrown off by a submarine's periscope. It spread further, and a broad trail of foam appeared behind it. Then a slim, dark sail rose out of the foam, and seconds later Devilfish was on the surface. She was already slowing down as the helicopter turned toward her.

Cappel stood up and began to make his way one step at a time toward the door. The winchman was already getting the sling ready to lower. Cappel grinned again. He wanted to see how Johnny was. And he couldn't help wondering what Johnny's face would look like when he heard what his next mission was.

The roar and whistle of the hovering helicopter nearly blew away Cheever's words as he stepped out onto Devilfish's main deck. He had to shout to get through to Frank Bronson.

"I said—Cappel hasn't told me why we're flying up to Washington. All he said was it's urgent."

Bronson laughed. "I know. That covers a multitude

11

of sins. Don't sweat it, sir. Any particular instructions?"

Cheever shook his head and reached up a hand to wedge his hat more firmly on his head. "No. Standard routine for docking and the rest."

"What about leave?"

Cheever frowned. With a crew like *Devilfish*'s there was never any point in being cheap about liberty and leave. *Devilfish*'s crew could be trusted to be on hand when there was work to be done. But there were such things as circumstances beyond the best man's control. And with the apparent possibility of a new mission coming up—

Cheever shook his head. "Not until I find out what Cappel's up to. That shouldn't be more than a day or two. Tell the crew that we may have to go to sea again in a hurry."

Bronson nodded. "I will. I suspect that's nothing less than the truth, too."

Cheever started to reply, then looked up to see the sling dropping down from the helicopter. It came to a stop almost in front of him, swinging back and forth in the gentle breeze. He grabbed the hand grips and thrust his legs one at a time into the canvas loops. Then he waved a hand to the winchman above. The sling began to rise, and simultaneously the helicopter swung away from *Devilfish*. Cheever was whisked past the sail only a few feet above the periscope standards; then he was out over the sea. A moment later the helicopter's cabin door loomed in front of him, with the winchman reaching out a hand to help him up. Behind the winchman Cheever saw the square, white-fringed face of Admiral Cappel.

As soon as Cheever had untangled himself from the sling, he looked closely at Admiral Cappel. He was trying to see if the admiral had changed any in the two months since they'd last seen each other. Apparently not. There might be one or two more lines in the bulldog face and one or two fewer hairs in the white thatch. But the wide gray eyes were as lively as ever, the handshake just as firm, the heavy frame just as erect and steady on wide-splayed legs.

"Hello, Johnny," said the admiral. "Welcome back."

"Thank you, sir."

The admiral motioned them to seats. "How's our girl?"

Cheever knew he was referring to *Devilfish*, not to anything human—except that to a sailor his ship almost is human.

"She's as much of a dream as ever, sir," he said with a broader smile than usual. He couldn't keep satisfaction with *Devilfish* off his face or out of his voice if he tried. Usually he didn't try.

Cappel nodded. "Would you recommend declaring her operational?"

Cheever didn't have to hesitate. "I would. And every man on board would back me up." His long face creased in another brief smile. "I think the crew would damned near mutiny if we didn't get accepted for operational service."

"Good," said Cappel. "Damned good." He leaned back as much as the seat allowed. "I don't mind telling you, Johnny, that your opinion is enough for me. I don't care what it means in the Pentagon, where they don't know you. We'll go ahead on your say-so and worry about getting the proper forms filled out later."

Cheever was tempted to ask, "Go ahead with what?" In fact, he almost had to bite his lip to keep from throwing out the question. But he kept his peace. There was no point in trying to pump the admiral if he didn't want to be pumped. Cappel certainly looked like a bluff and hearty seadog, and he might even think of himself as one. But he was a master negotiator, and there was no getting around that. It was a talent that had made him worth his weight in refined plutonium

13

to a long succession of superior officers, going all the way back to World War II and the first days of the atomic submarine project under Rickover himself.

So he sat in silence and watched *Devilfish* shrink until she was only a dot on the sea. Then even that dot faded out and the helicopter was alone in the twilight.

They flew in over the eastern shore of Virginia, then headed on up Chesapeake Bay. Cheever watched the lights of the Norfolk-Newport News area fade away behind them into the darkness. The sun was only a faint glow on the western horizon now, and the water a thousand feet below was dark except for the occasional lights of yachts or freighters.

They flew on north and reached the point where Cheever expected them to turn west, toward Washington. Instead, the helicopter turned east, toward the Maryland eastern shore. Cheever raised his eyebrows and looked a question at the admiral. Cappel didn't say anything.

The helicopter flew in from the bay, over a broad river mouth. Cheever recognized it as the mouth of the Choptank River. The moon had risen now, and he could see the line where silvered water gave way to dark land.

They crossed that line. A moment later the helicopter started to descend, sliding down rapidly. Cheever wondered if the pilot knew what he was doing, going down this fast in dark and unknown country.

Then lights blazed ahead. Through the cockpit windows Cheever could see a ring of floodlights outlining a concrete helipad. It looked clean and shiny, as though it had just been built. Again Cheever looked at Cappel, but the admiral's face was expressionless. Apparently he was determined to play the mystery through to the end.

The helicopter settled down with a bump, the en-

14

gine whine died, and the rotors whick-whick-whicked to a stop. Cappel motioned Cheever toward the door. The two men climbed out onto the helipad.

As they stepped away from the helicopter, Cheever saw a tall, burly black man in a laboratory coat approaching them. He came up and nodded to Admiral Cappel.

Cappel's expressionless face finally split in a grin.

"Johnny, this is Commander Lerone McNeil. He's in charge of developing the equipment for your first operational mission."

"I'm very happy to meet you, Commander," said Cheever. "I've been wondering about what was in store for us all the way from the Azores."

McNeil acknowledged the greeting with another jerk of his head, then led the way off the helipad in silence. It wasn't until they were climbing up a winding hillside path that McNeil turned to Cheever and spoke.

"It's a bold project, Commander. I think you'll agree on that. Basically you'll be taking *Devilfish* on a three-month voyage without any food on board."

## 3

A sudden silence descended on the three men. Cappel's face was unreadable, while McNeil's looked almost gleeful. Cheever kept his own face expressionless. He didn't feel like giving the scientist the satisfaction of even suspecting he had scored a point. But behind his expressionless face, his thoughts were racing.

Was McNeil making an elaborate joke? Or was his preposterous statement a shorthand way of describing something worth taking seriously? Cheever decided it had to be the latter. Otherwise he'd have to assume that Cappel was a party to the joke. He'd believe that when he saw water run uphill.

So when Cheever replied, he matched his tone and smile to McNeil's. "That is a bold project, Commander. I agree with you. But aren't you overlooking something? My men do need some food. 'Ask not how ye shall be fed or clothed' was a good idea two thousand years ago, I suppose. *Devilfish* is air conditioned, so no doubt we can work in our skins. But I don't see how we can get around the food problem. I know the prophet Elijah was fed by ravens in the desert, and I suppose seagulls could do the same. But how will they get to us when we're running submerged—"

At this point Admiral Cappel threw back his head and let out a roar of hearty, triumphant laughter that must have been heard on the other side of the Choptank River. He went on laughing until he was out of breath, then gasped and wheezed. Finally he ran down into silence and looked from McNeil to Cheever and back again.

McNeil was looking more annoyed than anything else. Cappel apparently found that amusing too. For a moment it looked to Cheever as though the admiral was going to go off into more gales of laughter. But he fought down the impulse.

"I warned you, Commander," he said. "Don't say I didn't warn you. I told you Johnny could give as good as he got, or better."

"So you did," said McNeil. The annoyance was off his face now, but his smile looked a little uncertain. "Anyway, what I said was very much a shorthand way

16

of describing the project. There will be plenty of food on board, but most of it will be made as you go along."

They walked on up the path as McNeil explained what was in the works for *Devilfish*. Gradually Cheever lost many of his initial doubts about the scientist. He certainly knew his own field, and as for the rest of him—well, Cheever was a firm believer in the adage "It takes all kinds." He didn't necessarily want all kinds aboard *Devilfish*, of course, but otherwise—why worry?

"You know, of course, that all the various nutrients the human body needs are compounded by nature out of a limited range of elements," McNeil began.

Cheever nodded. "That's basic chemistry. Even Annapolis teaches that."

There was a fizzing sound from Admiral Cappel, like a leaking soft drink bottle. He was obviously trying hard not to laugh again. This time McNeil ignored him and went on explaining.

"A few years ago it became possible to produce synthetic protein, fit for human consumption—"

"More or less," put in Cappel.

"The whole world can't afford T-bone steaks, sir," said McNeil. His eyes were hard. Cheever mentally gave the scientist low marks for tact and waited for Cappel to explode. But the admiral apparently was used to McNeil's manners. He let the interruption go and the rebuke pass.

"Anyway," McNeil went on, "the Japanese are now producing synthetic protein for human consumption by letting algae cultures work on crude oil. It's also possible to produce a full range of carbohydrates by slight variations in the process. Since we've been able to synthesize most vitamins for years, we can now provide a completely balanced human diet from synthetics.

"That's step one, and it's an important step. All by

itself, it may mean the difference between full bellies and starvation for millions of people. But the synthetic food plants now are the size of factories. The culture vats are the size of oil-storage tanks, and everything else is in proportion.

"What we're in the middle of now is step two. Suppose we could get the size of one of those plants down by a factor of three or four? Then we could fit it in a two-room apartment—or a submarine."

There was another silence. Cheever realized that this time McNeil wasn't playing any games. He was waiting for a serious reply and deserved one.

"It would be an enormously important breakthrough," said Cheever quietly. "The modern atomic submarine is already a closed system for air and water. If she could be made a closed system for food—"

If that were possible, an atomic submarine could cruise as long as her crew and her equipment could stand the strain. Cheever remembered the story of *Triton*, the huge atomic submarine that had made a submerged trip around the world in 1961. With practically every spare inch of room in her huge hull crammed with food, she had been able to pack in only enough for 120 days. And more recent submarines had nowhere near as much spare room. You could stuff in just so many bags and boxes before the crew became unable to reach their stations or the controls.

But if a submarine could manufacture her own food as she cruised along—

Cheever grinned. "There was a joke when the *Nautilus* was launched, back in 1954. They said an atomic submarine would have to come into port only often enough for the crew to reenlist. If this—idea—works out, that won't be a joke any more."

"Exactly," said McNeil. "That's the whole idea behind the project. It's the first major scientific research job that the Office of Special Submarine Operations is

18

handling, and if we can bring it off, it won't be the last."

"Provided Senator Bergen doesn't succeed in getting us cut out of the Navy's research and development budget for next year," put in the admiral.

"Is there any danger of that?" said Cheever. "I thought—"

Cappel raised a warning hand for silence. Cheever looked ahead and saw that the path ended at a gate in a high wire fence. Lights on tall steel poles stood at intervals just inside the fence but gave no illumination. Beyond the fence Cheever made out the shadowy form of one of the old Colonial mansions that studded Maryland's eastern shore.

As the three officers approached the gate, two very large men materialized out of the sentry box to the left of the gate. They wore dark coveralls, but they carried .45s and M-16s and they carried themselves like combat veterans. Ex-Marines, Cheever suspected. They also wore heavy goggles.

The two men saluted and held out their hands. Cappel pulled out his ID, and Cheever and McNeil did the same. One of the men shone a dimmed flashlight on all three cards, then nodded to his companion. The other opened the gate and motioned the officers through. The speed, the silence, and the way the men moved with total assurance in almost total darkness made the whole sequence rather eerie.

It wasn't until they were halfway up the path to the house that Cheever remembered the goggles and put two and two together.

"Why is everything under infrared, Commander?" he asked McNeil.

"It does just as well for showing up intruders," said the scientist. "And it doesn't attract as much attention from our neighbors or casual passersby. If we had regular floodlights all around, the place would be visible for miles and God knows what the locals would think."

"Is the whole place guarded like this?"

Cappel grimaced. "Score another for Senator Bergen. We could only squeeze out enough money to put in full security around Complex One—the laboratory and workshops. Most of our people either commute or live in an unsecured house a couple of miles over that way." He jerked his thumb off to the left. "It's a stupid setup. If anybody ever gets curious about what we're doing here, it'll be too damned easy to snatch one of our people. I don't like it one damned bit, and one of these days I'm going to lay it right on Senator Bergen, even if the CNO won't."

They walked the rest of the way to the house in silence. There were two more sentries at the main door. Then they found themselves in a richly paneled, brightly lit entry hall. At the foot of the winding, formal staircase a pretty, freckle-faced blonde woman sat behind a large mahogany desk half covered with telephones and switches.

"Hi, Connie," said Cappel.

"Good evening, sir," the receptionist replied. "Doctor McNeil, Commander—?"

"John Cheever," said Cappel. He didn't volunteer any more information. Cheever decided to follow the admiral's lead.

"You'll be wanting the workshop, right?" said Connie.

Cappel nodded, and she pressed one of the switches. In the distance a bell tinkled loudly, and nearer at hand there was the click of a door opening. Cappel led the way around the staircase to where a rosewood paneled door stood ajar. Beyond it was a brightly lit flight of stairs leading down out of sight.

"The fortunes of the family that built this house in 1745 were founded on large-scale smuggling," said Cappel as he led them down the stairs. "So they equipped it with nice big cellars and a whole network of tunnels running under the whole estate, where they could store and hide brandy, tobacco, and so on. They built big and they built well. You'd need a five-hundred-pound bomb to break in from the outside. And we've added electronic surveillance, listening devices, sleep gas—the works. Nobody's going to do anything down here. If our people topside weren't such sitting ducks—"

He broke off as they reached the bottom of the stairs, where they still had another pair of sentries to get through. Finally they headed down a brick-lined passageway that ended in a massive and unmistakably modern steel door. McNeil opened the door and led the others into the room beyond.

Cheever's first impression was that McNeil had filled the white-painted basement room with a series of giant coffee boilers. Then he noticed the maze of pipes connecting the gleaming metal cylinders and revised his impression to a surrealistic octopus. Or maybe two of them, making love?

When it came to actually showing off his work, McNeil was in his element. He strode around the machinery, rapping out statistics and design features as fast and fluently as a computer, pointing out this or that technical innovation. Some of them were his own, and he was not backward in claiming them. But when something had been contributed by someone else, he was just as ready to put the credit where it was due. Sometimes he bent down and shoe-horned his enormous frame in among the pipes and cylinders to point something out or make minute adjustments. McNeil's hands were enormous, but the movements of their long fingers were surprisingly light and delicate.

Finally he stepped back and turned to the others. "Basically, the whole thing breaks down into three parts. Reception—that takes in the raw materials—$CO_2$

from the atmosphere and any sort of organic matter, including garbage and sewage. Treatment—where it's filtered and sterilized. Culturation—where the algae go to work. And finally processing—where the various compounds are turned into edible substances. Eventually we expect to have the machinery perfected to the point where it can treat things like plankton and seaweed. We're designing a plankton strainer that can be fitted to submarines and—"

"Let's not get ahead of ourselves," said Cappel gently. "One thing at a time."

McNeil nodded and even smiled. "Quite right, sir. That's for the Mark III or maybe the Mark IV processor. This one here is the Mark I—the pilot model. With it, we've proved that the processor works. Admiral, what's doing at your end with the Mark II?"

Cappel took his cue. "The first Mark II—the operational model—is in Baltimore getting its final tests. As soon as the tests are completed, we'll be sending it down to Norfolk and installing it on board Devilfish."

Cheever had seen that coming. But loyalty to his crew compelled him to put in a word. "Why Devilfish, sir?"

"Because she's the only sub where we can install the equipment without ripping out several million dollars' worth of essential gear," said Cappel. He looked at Cheever. "Or isn't that the problem?"

Cheever looked at the admiral, then at McNeil. He hoped the scientist wouldn't react the wrong way, but he had to say it. "Frankly, sir, I'm thinking of the crew. How long are they going to have to—if I may say so—eat their own shit?"

Cappel laughed. "Don't worry, Johnny. There's going to be plenty of ordinary food on board too. It's a test of the processor, not your crew's stomachs."

"That's good," said Cheever. "But I'd still like to know how long we're going to be at sea. We weren't

22

expecting another long trip right after our shakedown."

Cappel nodded. "Good point. Plans are still flexible, but you won't be at sea more than—oh, ninety days or so. However, Commander McNeil's an optimist. He's calling the test Operation Endless Voyage."

4

As the helicopter slipped out over the water, Cappel turned to Cheever.

"Well, Johnny. What's your reaction? Personal, unofficial, no punches pulled."

"Is that an order, sir?"

Cappel laughed. "Since when have you needed an order to speak without pulling any punches? I don't think you were mealy-mouthed even as a plebe at the Academy."

"All right, sir. I think it's a magnificent idea. I think *Devilfish* can bring it off, and I doubt if any other submarine could. If we do bring it off it will mean a lot to the submarine force, and to other people as well."

"Are you thinking of the space program?"

"You read my mind, sir. Yes. The processor would be the answer to NASA's dream for a space station or a trip to Mars."

"It would be," said Cappel. "In fact, that's why there's NASA money in Endless Voyage. Very much under the counter, and irregularly enough so that half a dozen heads will roll for misappropriation of funds if

23

it ever comes out. But very much there. It's already saved us a year's development time, and it may turn out to have saved the whole processor project, if Bergen hits us this year."

"How likely is that, sir?"

"Too damned likely. Bergen has got the notion into his head that we're a CIA front. And that means that we deserve to get the axe. It's a way of scoring cheap points with the voters back home."

"Are we clear of the CIA, sir?" Cheever's voice was cool. He was a career naval officer, not a spy or a man who worked for spies. He wanted to keep it that way.

"There's no way to give an iron-clad guarantee on that, Johnny," said Cappel. "But I'm damned sure of one thing—if there's anybody from the Agency at O.S.S.O., he's pulling his weight in the job he's doing for us. If he does that, I'm not going to worry about whatever else he does. A man my age has only so much time left for worrying and I'll be damned if I'll waste any of it on what can't be helped. All right?"

"All right, sir."

They were halfway across the bay before Cheever spoke again. "Are my crew going to be trained to operate the processor? Or is McNeil sending a team along to run it?"

"He was planning on coming along himself, with a team of four," said Cappel. "Why?"

"I was thinking. If the technicians have to come along, Bergen can always say the processor needs more development."

Cappel nodded. "No money for procurement."

"Exactly, sir. But if our own crew can operate it, it will look like a much better proposition. Maybe not good enough to convince Bergen himself, but sufficient to convince some of his colleagues so they'll sit on him."

Cappel looked thoughtful. "Good point, Johnny."

More silence. "Does this have anything to do with—Commander McNeil himself?"

It was Cheever's turn to be silent. Then he said, picking his words carefully, "It does, partly. Other things being equal, I'd rather not have McNeil himself aboard *Devilfish* on a long submerged voyage."

"Problems with your crew?"

Cheever shook his head. "Not directly. It's McNeil himself. He doesn't come across as the type of man to keep his head in a tight spot or who gets along with people very well. You know better than I do how important those things are aboard a submarine, where you're rubbing elbows with everybody all the time whether you like it or not. Little vices start looking big, and big ones can cause real trouble. McNeil would probably be unpopular aboard *Devilfish*, maybe to the point where I'd have to take steps with the crew."

"Um." Cappel frowned. "Do you think—let's be blunt about it—McNeil's race has anything to do with it?"

Cheever felt himself on solid ground there. "No, sir, it does not. At least not aboard *Devilfish*. She has a picked crew, and I would say there's not a man of them who would raise an eyebrow at a man with three heads and a purple tail if he *did his job*. That's the problem, sir. The crew won't be sure that McNeil isn't dead weight, and possibly unstable emotionally. And frankly, neither will I."

"Sorry, Johnny. But I had to ask. If there was even one little racial incident over McNeil's being on board, Bergen would have our balls barbecued for lunch the day after it hit the papers. He loves that sort of issue. Not because he loves any of the people involved, but because he loves headlines."

"He's a politician," said Cheever. "What more can you expect?"

25

Commander McNeil turned out the workshop lights, made sure that all the lights on the security-system monitoring board were green, then closed the door behind him and went upstairs.

"Good night, Connie," he said as he passed the receptionist's desk.

She smiled. She had the kind of face that a smile seemed to light up from within. "Good night, Doctor McNeil."

McNeil was smiling too as he let himself out through the main door. If he had a choice, he preferred to be called "Doctor" rather than "Commander." He was prouder of his competence in marine engineering, his brilliance in marine biology, than he was of his reserve navy commission. That commission was an accident, almost a gift given to him to make it easier for him to work on Navy projects that he hadn't really wanted to work on anyway. At least O.S.S.O. was showing some promise in the scientific line. It would be worth staying here, even if there were ex-Marines everywhere and admirals and their friends looking over his shoulder. And he supposed he'd have to get used to being called "Commander" if it made the blue-and-gold boys more comfortable—why not?

He was so busy thinking the matter over that he missed the fork in the path. One fork—the one he took—led down to the helipad and beyond that to the shore. The other—the one he had meant to take—led off to the left, to the other house and the cottage where the staff lived.

McNeil turned back up the path and looked for the fork. God, it was dark out here. Instinctively he tightened his grip on the briefcase handcuffed to his right wrist. The handcuff chafed. He stopped to unlock it and take it off. More damned cloak-and-dagger nonsense!

He took a few more steps; then suddenly there was a

gap in the trees and bushes off to his right. The faint white gleam of the gravel path curved away into the darkness. He stopped and started to turn.

He had turned halfway around when he heard the cracking of bushes and the sound of running feet behind him. Reflexes developed in football and skin diving made him spin around to face the approaching footsteps. He dropped into a crouch, swinging the briefcase up to use as a shield. Damn! He should have taken Sergeant Gonzales' advice and brought his .45. Not that he could ever hit anything with it, but—

Before he could complete the thought, the attackers were on him.

There were two of them, dressed in black, with black stocking caps over their heads and black gloves on their hands. One of them swung around to McNeil's left, trying to get behind him, while the other came at him from the front. Something gleamed dully in the second man's hand.

But McNeil had been an all-American fullback at the University of Michigan. He had known then and remembered now what to do with a man coming at you from behind. He sidestepped as fast as he had ever done in the stadium, then kicked out hard behind him. He felt his foot slam into something solid and heard the attacker gasp. But he didn't go down, and McNeil felt hands close around his foot and ankle, pulling him off balance. He twisted as he fell, to avoid landing helplessly on his back or breaking anything. Simultaneously, he clutched at the feet and ankles of the man in front of him.

The man was bending over as McNeil grabbed, the gleaming object in his right hand descending toward the back of the scientist's neck. But he was a small man, and he didn't expect to suddenly find himself grabbed around the ankles by two hundred and forty pounds of ex-all American. McNeil jerked hard, and the man lost his balance and began to go over backward. As he did, he threw out his hands in a desperate effort to keep his balance. The gleaming object flew out of his hand and sailed into the bushes. The man landed on the path with a thud and a grunt.

Then McNeil felt the man behind him scrambling up on top of him, trying to get a choke hold. McNeil was not a wrestler and never had been, but he did have a very thick neck with more muscle in it than the attacker had counted on. McNeil jerked his head forward, then lurched to his feet, taking the man with him, simultaneously aiming an elbow backward. He aimed the elbow where he guessed the man's groin would be, and his guess was correct. He felt the man's hands loosen from his neck, and heard him let out an ear-splitting scream of agony.

That reminded McNeil that perhaps he'd better do a little shouting too and get some help. As the second man fell off him and crumpled up in a moaning heap on the ground, McNeil took a deep breath and let out a yell.

"Help! Help! HELLLLLLLLLPPPP!"

It was a yell that would have wakened the long-dead McClarys in their family vault, but it also alerted the live guards at the main house. Before the yell had died away, McNeil saw the floodlights around the main house coming on—blink, blink, flare. A siren sounded, and from the helipad a red rocket shot up into the sky.

The man in front of McNeil stiffened at the sound. His eyes roamed around and spotted the fallen briefcase. He dived for it. So did McNeil. But the attacker got there first. He snatched it up under one arm and leaped for the bushes. McNeil plunged after him.

He was almost up with the man when the other drew a small automatic from his pocket and fired twice at point-blank range. McNeil yelled again, as one bullet lashed the side of his face and his ear and the other

28

stung his ribs. He stopped, then dropped flat on the ground and started to roll toward the bushes.

But he didn't need to make for cover. The man had shaken off his most dangerous pursuer, and that was enough. Shoving the gun back into his pocket, he vanished into the undergrowth. Bushes crackled and twigs snapped behind him for a moment; then even that sound died away as he plunged off into the distance.

McNeil groaned and raised a cautious hand to the side of his face. He could feel the gouge through the flesh of his cheek and the cartilage of his right ear and the blood flowing down. It would hurt like hell. In fact, it was beginning to hurt like hell already, as the shock wore off. And it was going to mean another scar. But street fights and football practice, let alone football games, had given him worse.

Then he felt cautiously at his side, and there too he felt gouged flesh and oozing blood and a growing pain that sharpened each time he breathed. He decided not to take off his coat to examine the wound. There might be a broken rib, and if so—

He had just reached that decision when clumping footsteps and flashing lights told him that the guards were finally coming. "Hallllooooo!" he shouted. "It's McNeil. I'm here!"

There were answering shouts from all along three paths, and a moment later guards dashed up. Sergeant Gonzales was leading the four men from Complex One, all with their M-16s held ready. They looked extremely well armed, extremely tough, and extremely competent. For a moment McNeil felt a good deal warmer about things military than he ever had before. He was lucky—damned lucky—to be alive.

"What happened, sir?" said Gonzales.

"Two men jumped me. One got the briefcase and got away. He took a couple of shots at me as he left. I—"

"*Nombre de Dios!*" exclaimed the sergeant, as he shone the light on McNeil's bloody face. "Waskow! Get the first-aid kit. Murger, go call the doctor. On the double!" Two of the guards vanished. "The rest of you—team up and start searching the grounds. Try to take prisoners if possible. But if you are shot at, shoot to kill." The men strode away, their faces grim and businesslike.

Gonzales turned back to McNeil. "What about the other one, sir?"

"He's around here somewhere," said McNeil. A ghost of a smile played across his face. "I put an elbow in his balls, so I don't think he got very—"

A shout came from out of the bushes. "Hey, Sarge, we've found one of them!"

Gonzales spun around. "If he's alive, be—"

"Never mind, Sarge," said the same voice. "He's *real* dead. Must have took something, looks like."

Gonzales went over to look, and a moment later McNeil heard a good deal of Spanish cursing coming out of the bushes. He was finding it hard to pay attention to what was going on around him, though. The pain was still mounting, and it was beginning to build a wall between him and the world.

At that point Waskow arrived with the first-aid kit. McNeil extended his arm for the morphine shot, and breathed a sigh of relief as it began slowly nibbling away at the pain.

The corridors of the Pentagon were sterile, echoing, and empty under the lights as Cappel led Cheever to the O.S.S.O. offices. They lay well down in the bowels of the huge building, within easy reach of the office of the Chief of Naval Operations. They were far beyond the "Authorized Personnel Only" doors with their security checks and sober-faced guards.

Cappel led Cheever into the outer room of the offices, then stopped abruptly. The red "Urgent" light on the base of the telephone was glowing. Cappel picked up the receiver and punched the button for the operator.

"Hello, Cappel here. What's the trouble?" A moment's silence. "Gonzales at Complex One? Emergency? Thank you." He cut out the operator, then punched another number and the button for the scrambler.

A moment later he said, "Hello, Sergio. You've got a problem?" Then the admiral stiffened. Cheever saw the smile leave his face. He stood up, still holding on to the receiver, and his eyes focused on some spot far beyond the blue-painted walls of the office. Cheever felt a momentary chill. Something was badly wrong, something important enough to bring the admiral to full alert. Cappel must have looked very much like this as he stood at the periscope of *Stonefish*, driving her in against a Japanese convoy.

For the next couple of minutes, Cheever would have given a good deal to be on an extension line. The admiral's clipped phrases let out only tantalizing hints of the other half of the conversation. "Two of them—one took poison—McNeil's not hurt?—*what?*" There was a moment when it looked as though the admiral were making a heroic effort to get his temper under control. Then, "No, Sergio, I'm not blaming you. If we had more men or a better security system—yes, everybody's to go armed. What? Well, see that they get it if they don't have it already. Meanwhile, I'll call the FBI right away. Thanks, Sergio, and well done. Now for God's sake relax." Cappel's large hand clenched so tight that the knuckles stood out. He put the receiver back in its cradle. Then he seemed to relax as he turned toward Cheever.

"Somebody tried to do a body-snatch on Commander McNeil between Complex One and the

31

residence. Two of them, apparently professionals. They were going to shoot him full of come-along drugs, but apparently he got wind of the attack somehow and fought them off."

Cheever's eyebrows rose skeptically. "Don't let that lab coat and the Ph.D. fool you, Johnny. McNeil comes from the worst part of the Detroit ghetto, and if he hadn't learned about dirty fighting back then he wouldn't be here today. Then he was an all-American fullback at Michigan, while he was pulling down straight A's as a biochemistry major. Since then he's kept himself in first-class trim with running and skin diving. He's one tough customer, and apparently those two snatchers didn't expect anybody like him." For a moment the admiral looked almost cheerful. "Anyway, he fought them off. Crippled one, drove the other away. But the one that got away did snatch McNeil's briefcase. And the one he crippled suicided before Gonzales' men found him."

Cheever grimaced. "What was in the briefcase?"

"Gonzales didn't know. He'll have to ask McNeil, and right now McNeil's under sedation. The one that got away creased him twice with a .32. Nothing serious, but he's hurting like hell, and the doctors have put him out for a few hours. Meanwhile they're looking for the second man. Gonzales has called the Maryland State Police, and I'm going to get the FBI on it right now."

Cappel picked up the telephone again. With only short intervals, he was on it for the next half hour. He talked to people from the FBI, the CNO's office, the National Security Council, the Maryland State Police, and several others that Cheever couldn't identify from the admiral's end of the conversation. Finally Cappel put the receiver back for the last time and sat down in the leather swivel chair with a long, gusty sigh of relief. Then he unlocked a drawer in his desk and pulled out a bottle of Irish whiskey and two glasses. He filled each glass with about four fingers of the pale, gold-brown whiskey, then handed one glass to Cheever.

"I don't know whether to pat McNeil on the back or kick him in the ass over this," Cappel said.

"What did he do?"

"He wasn't wearing his sidearm, that's what he didn't do! If he'd been able to put a .45 slug into each of those characters—! Oh well, if they catch the second one, no damage done. But everybody who works at Complex One is going to go armed from now on. If they don't know how to use a gun already, Gonzales has orders to teach them at least which end the bullet comes out of!"

Cappel drained off about half the whiskey at one swig, then went on. "This business is *bad* news, whether we get the briefcase back or not. The opposition obviously has a notion that the Complex is something important, even if they don't know exactly what. Very important. They don't risk their good illegals— their field agents—for peanuts. Good men don't grow on bushes for them any more than they do for us, Besides, there's always more risk of scandal and exposure for them in the U.S. than there is for us in Russia. That's one advantage the newspapers give us, even if they screw up a lot of other things." He drained the rest of the whiskey.

Cheever sipped at his glass. "Does this involve any change of plans for *Devilfish*, sir?"

Cappel pulled at one cheek as he considered the matter. Finally he said, "I don't think so. At least not for the moment."

"Then can I authorize Frank Bronson to go ahead with issuing leave permits and picking the men for training on the processor?"

"Sure, Johnny."

"Thank you, sir." Cheever rose, set his glass down

33

on the desk, and reached for the telephone. As his hand came down on the receiver, the telephone rang. He picked up the receiver.

"Hello, Admiral Cappel's office?" came the voice on the line.

"Yes."

"Is the admiral available? It is Sergeant Gonzales. We have another emer—"

Before the sergeant had finished the last word, Cheever thrust the telephone at Cappel. The admiral listened in silence for a minute, but his face turned hard and grim as he listened. Looking at Cappel, Cheever could almost feel the temperature in the office dropping.

Finally the admiral hung up, and there was a moment of equally chilly silence. Then—

"They found the second man. He tried to fight it out, and one of the guards chopped him up with an M-16. He's DOA. But he didn't have the briefcase. Not on him, not anywhere around him. They're searching for it, but I'm going to alert the Coast Guard. Just in case."

Another moment's silence. Cheever braced himself. He knew that something bad was coming. He had been around Cappel long enough to know the admiral's moods and what these silences meant.

"In any case, we've got to assume that O.S.S.O. and *Devilfish* are compromised. McNeil said there was a complete schema for the installation of the processor in *Devilfish* in the briefcase. If the opposition puts a good technical man on it, they'll be able to figure out one hell of a lot. Too much."

He looked at Cheever, with affectionate regret in the gray eyes under the thick white brows. "This does screw things up for *Devilfish*. We're going to have to get Operation Endless Voyage underway as soon as possible. Otherwise, we may wind up with another snatch attempt, or sabotage of *Devilfish*, or a leak to the papers intended to prove we're doing something undercover. Then listen to Bergen yell!

"So I'm afraid there's not going to be any leave for your crew, and no training either. It will take about ten days to install the Mark II processor and patch up McNeil to the point where he can work with it aboard *Devilfish*. I want *Devilfish* to be ready for sea at the end of those ten days."

Cheever was silent for a moment. He considered what his men would say. He considered what Bronson would say. He considered what he owed to them and to his magnificent ship.

Then he said what he had said in reply to orders since he entered Annapolis many years before.

"Aye aye, sir."

5

In the dockyard shack in Norfolk, Frank Bronson was talking on the telephone.

"Yes, sir—full cooperation—of course, sir. What—? I suppose so, but— Yes, I know. Can do, sir."

He hung up and turned to Chief Machinist's Mate Peter "Fishman" Nielsen. Nielsen was known as "Fishman" from having done most of his twenty-one years of service in underwater demolitions or submarines. He was a barrel-chested Minnesotan more than six feet tall and nearly six feet wide. He was also Chief of the

Boat—senior enlisted man aboard *Devilfish*—and by custom if not by law adviser and counselor to both the commanding officer and the executive officer. In the years since beards became allowable in the United States Navy, he had grown a luxuriant blond one. With a horned helmet on his head and a sword or battleaxe in his hand, he could have stepped aboard any Viking ship that ever sailed with no questions asked.

Right now the part of his tanned face that was visible above the beard was twisted in a questioning frown. As Bronson hung up, Nielsen cleared his throat.

"Trouble, sir?"

Bronson nodded. "That was the CO on the line. No leaves, civilian techs coming on board to install some new equipment, and we're supposed to be ready for sea in ten days."

Nielsen was silent for a moment. Then he said, "Damn." That from Nielsen was the equivalent of twenty minutes of fluent profanity from anyone less soft-spoken.

Bronson sighed. "I know. We all had thirty days at home dancing in our heads. I had promised to take the kids down to Cape May for a week, and now Becky'll have my hide. I don't suppose I was the only one with plans like that, either."

"No, sir, you weren't," said Nielsen.

Bronson shrugged. "Damn again. But if the captain says it can't be done, it can't be done." He picked up his hat. "I'd better get back on board and call a meeting in the wardroom. Can you take care of breaking the news to the crew?"

"Aye aye, sir."

Bronson thought of adding, "And handling any trouble so it doesn't get to me or on the man's record." But with *Devilfish*'s crew he didn't expect there would be any trouble of that sort. And if there was, Fishman

36

knew how to handle it without being told. Giving him that sort of advice would be an insult.

He put on his hat, squared it away in the glass window of the phone booth, and led the way out of the shack. The lights on the roof of the covered drydock reflected in the black water that lapped around *Devilfish*'s even blacker hull. In the dim light, Bronson had a stronger feeling than usual that the submarine was a living creature. A living creature, confined for the moment, but eager for release into the open seas that were her only true home. He could almost sense that the ship was sneering at the weakness of the men who manned her.

He put the fantasies firmly out of his mind and led the way across the gangplank onto *Devilfish*'s deck.

"You can go in now, sir," said the nurse, a fresh-faced lieutenant jg.

"Thank you," said Cheever, and opened the door. Inside the white-painted hospital room Lerone McNeil sat propped up in bed, bare to the waist. The bandages on cheek and abdomen were startlingly white against his heavy, dark features and massively muscled dark torso.

"Good morning, Commander," said Cheever. "How are you feeling?"

McNeil shrugged, then winced as the incautious movement strained the wound in his side. "Pretty comfortable, all things considered. As I told that Marine who patched me up—where I came from, you can pick up worse than this going down to the corner for a loaf of bread—if you can afford the bread. I stayed, then left on my feet. Sissies got out or got under." There was a flat challenge in McNeil's voice, defying Cheever to comment on him or his background.

Cheever decided to let the challenge pass. As he had said to Admiral Cappel, he didn't care if a man had three heads and a purple tail—or where he came from, or what he had done when he was young. And he'd bet his Annapolis class ring that nobody aboard *Devilfish* would care either. The problem was McNeil's state of mind.

"So I gather," said Cheever after a short silence. "Admiral Cappel told me a good deal about you."

"He did?" There was no mistaking the suspicion in McNeil's voice. Cheever wondered what the scientist might be thinking that Cappel had said about him. Then he decided to take the bull by the horns.

"He gave me a rundown on your life," said Cheever. "It impressed me. It impressed the hell out of me, as a matter of fact. I didn't realize you were responsible for the Mark II deep diver. We've got two assigned to *Devilfish.* We'll probably be taking one of them on this mission."

"Good. And I can run one. I took a master's degree in marine engineering as well as my doctorate." That was not made as a boast but as a statement of fact. Since Cheever knew it was a fact, he said nothing about it.

Instead, he said, "Are you sure you're going to be in shape to even come along, let alone run a deep diver?"

McNeil's face hardened. From quite handsome in a rugged fashion, it suddenly became almost ugly. Here it comes, thought Cheever. We may not even get out to sea before the "racial incident" happens, if that look on McNeil's face means anything. But I owe it to my ship and crew to get the matter out into the open, no matter what McNeil—or Cappel—thinks of it.

"The doctor expects to have me out of here within a week," said McNeil. His voice was not angry, but it had no other sort of expression either. "And he expects I'd be completely fit within two weeks. I'm a quick healer, and he didn't think there could be any compli-

38

cations." He paused. "But that's not the question that's really on your mind, Commander. Is it?"

"No," said Cheever. "It isn't. The real question is whether you can cope with the situation aboard a submarine on a long-duration submerged cruise."

"What kind of situation?" said McNeil. His lips almost curled into a sneer. "Is your crew a bunch of rednecks?"

"They are not," said Cheever in a voice as chilly as McNeil's. "They are the best professionals in the United States Submarine Service. They won't have any doubts or worries about your skin color. But they may have others."

Cheever took a deep breath. "Doctor McNeil. You were born a man. Your talents and your education made you a brilliant scientist. The United States Navy made you an officer, more or less. But I don't know if any of them or all of them together have made you a man it would be safe to have aboard my ship. I don't know that they didn't, either. But I have to wonder and I have to ask. The only way I could stop doing that would be to step down as captain of *Devilfish*. The safety of his ship has been the captain's responsibility as long as there have been ships and captains."

McNeil had been practically holding his breath during Cheever's speech, his dark face turning darker. Now he let out the breath in a long, whistling sigh, then leaned back against the pillows. A good deal of tension went out of his body and face in a moment. When he spoke, it was obvious that some of it had also gone out of his mind. Not all, but at least some.

"All right, Commander Cheever," he said slowly. "I see what was bothering you. I didn't before. And I suppose you're right to worry. But why worry about me? I've made trips that lasted for months aboard oceanographic vessels, and I've been down in research subs for days at a time."

"I know," said Cheever. He hated to wither the olive branch that McNeil was holding out, but unfortunately he couldn't avoid it. "That doesn't prove you can cope with living cheek-by-jowl with sixty other men in a submarine submerged for weeks or months on end. And it's your peace of mind I'm worried about, more than anybody else's. My crew can cope with almost anything if they have to. They're trained. You aren't. You won't be much good for this project or for any other if you can't take the strain and suddenly fold up. And O.S.S.O. needs you, Doctor McNeil. It needs you sane and healthy, not in a hospital because you tried to prove you were tougher than men who've been trained for this work for up to twenty years."

Cheever was fighting to keep his face straight as he said this. He hadn't done so much "greasing" (flattery) on a difficult case since he'd been a division officer aboard *Muskallonge* ten years ago. There'd been a monumental problem child named Peabody, a sheer genius as a sonar man but a borderline alcoholic as well. Cheever had saved the man's navy career and even his submarine rating, but it had been touch-and-go for three months. Even thinking about it nearly gave Cheever ulcers. Facing the prospect of doing it again was even worse.

McNeil suddenly grinned disarmingly. "Commander, you've made your point again. I'm still coming with you, though, unless Admiral Cappel says otherwise. Do you think he's going to do that?"

Cheever shook his head.

"Okay, Commander. You may be right about my head. I don't think so, but you may be. Anyway, it is your ship. You're right about that. So don't worry about my trying to compete with your crew. If I feel that I can't handle things, I'll try to be as little trouble as possible until you can get me ashore. And I won't make any noise about it—unless somebody aboard *Devilfish* gives me a good reason."

"Fair enough, Doctor," said Cheever. He shook hands with McNeil, then went out. He felt relieved but still not quite happy. He had held out his own olive branch, and McNeil had taken it. But all the tension wasn't out of the situation.

Cheever sighed. It couldn't be out of the situation until it was out of McNeil. And the man's background made that damned near impossible!

That was unfortunate. McNeil was a brilliant and creative man, one that Cheever would respect under any circumstances. Beneath the scars of his childhood and youth, perhaps there was also a man Cheever could someday like.

## 6

Rain pattered down over Moscow, breaking the stifling summer heat and laying the dust in the parks and the streets. The green leaves of the trees along the street outside Admiral Barsukov's office windows shivered as the drops struck them.

With a quick, rough movement of his left arm, Barsukov jerked the curtains shut. He disliked Moscow weather, even at its best. It was soft, fit for bureaucrats, perhaps even for decadent Westerners. It was not fit for a man who had been born and raised within a few miles of the Arctic Circle and done most of his thirty years' service in the Soviet Arctic Fleet.

Thirty years' service, interrupted but not ended by the accident that had cost him his left arm. He sat down behind the big varnished desk and spread out both arms on the green blotter. The metal claw that served him as a left hand shone against the dark green. It was not pretty, but it had its uses. He picked up an empty ink bottle from the corner of the desk in the claw and flexed the massive muscles of his upper left arm and shoulder. There was a faint pop as the bottle disintegrated, and shards of glass sprayed over the blotter. He scooped them up on a piece of writing paper and dropped them into the wastebasket.

Thirty years' service, most of it spent on the bridges or in the control rooms of submarines, the silent and deadly defenders of the Soviet Arctic. It had not always been cold, though. It had been very hot aboard that ex-German submarine with the hydrogen peroxide engines when a fuel line broke. That was how he had lost his arm—thrusting it into the blazing fuel to turn a valve. The valve cut off the broken line and kept the flame from flowing back along it to detonate the main fuel tanks. Thirty-seven men owed their lives to his lost arm. For once the Soviet government had put its gratitude in useful form—promotion and rubles, as well as the gaudy gold star of a Hero of the Soviet Union.

But they had also tried to send him ashore for good. A one-armed man was no good aboard a submarine, they said. For two years he had fought to convince the big doctors otherwise. It had been a fight as hard as the time two German destroyers cornered him off the Norwegian coast and kept his little coastal sub pinned on the bottom for a whole day. But he had won the fight against the Germans, and in the end he had won the fight against the doctors too. If he had ever been

42

happier than the day he took a submarine out of Arch-angel again, he couldn't remember it.

But eventually age and the passage of time did what the doctors and the missing arm could not do. They had brought him ashore to stay, and even brought him to Moscow. Not that they had put him out of service even then. Now he lurked behind the title of Special Deputy to the Commander-in-Chief of the Soviet Navy. A very special deputy. When one of the Soviet Navy's four hundred submarines put to sea on any sort of special mission—espionage, terrorism, and the like— it sailed under Barsukov's orders. He worked directly with the C-in-C, at times with the Politburo, and some-times even with the KGB—the secret police. And he would be able to go on doing all of this for as long as he wished, as long as his mind and body held together. It was a position of great power, and in a land where the currency of success is raw power rather than money, he was a man to be envied.

But Barsukov in his turn envied those who still took their submarines out through drifting ice and the chill gray waves of the Arctic seas. He would go on envying them. But there was nothing he could do about that.

Since there was nothing he could do about it, he de-cided to spend no more time worrying about it. He reached for the wire "In" basket. He was just picking the top paper off the stack when the buzzer on his desk telephone sounded.

"Barsukov," he said.

It was his secretary. "Comrade Admiral, Captain Volynsky is here."

"Send him in."

The office door opened and Captain Leonid Vol-ynsky shuffled in. Barsukov looked at the man with a distaste that he was barely able to keep off his face. Volynsky shuffled because a man weighing one hundred and fifty kilograms finds it hard to walk normally. Barsukov found it hard to accept the notion of a man weighing one hundred and fifty kilograms as a naval officer. But Volynsky was a genius at intelligence work, and so indispensable that the Commander-in-Chief himself had ordered him promoted to captain. So there was nothing Barsukov could do about that, either.

Volynsky looked around the office for the strongest chair, found it, and sat down. It still creaked ominously under his weight, but it didn't dump him with a crash onto the floor. Barsukov had seen that happen in the past. Then he unpacked a sheaf of papers from his briefcase and spread them out on his lap. There was room on that lap for quite a lot of paper.

There was no point in hurrying Volynsky. Barsukov had learned that long ago. He waited until the intelligence expert had finished arranging the papers to his satisfaction. Then he cleared his throat.

"Well, Comrade Captain?"

"Comrade Admiral, I think I—we—have the right to draw some conclusions now. The latest material received through the KGB's illegal operations in America has been decisive."

"Very good. What are those conclusions?"

"The submarine named *Devilfish* is in fact a vessel of extremely advanced design and performance."

"How advanced?"

Volynsky looked annoyed. "That even I can't say. She is obviously designed to take various sorts of experimental equipment. Some of that equipment would have no purpose if she were not of particularly advanced design."

"Such as?"

"The only item we are certain of is a food-processing device, a compact machine for synthetic protein. This is in itself a major technical feat by—"

"Synthetic protein?" Barsukov asked. Then he

44

shook his head. "No, never mind the explanations. I'll take your word that it's important." If he gave Volynsky a chance to trot out his expertise, the man would be talking for an hour on this "food-processing device" alone before he went on to other and more important matters.

Again Volynsky looked annoyed at being cut off. Too bad. Barsukov didn't have any time to listen to the expert spout on like the whale he so much resembled. "What's the basis for your assumptions of advanced design?"

"A number of factors." Volynsky grinned, almost gloating. At last he had a chance to answer a question his own way, at his own length. "First, the material of *Devilfish* appears to be—"

It took fifteen minutes for Volynsky to sketch out his portrait of *Devilfish*. For once Barsukov did not find himself bored by the captain's long-windedness. A fiberglass submarine of radically unconventional design, with performance that no other submarine in the world could match. Barsukov had been aware for many years that the Americans had an overwhelming lead in the large-scale use of fiberglass, perhaps the ideal material for a deep-diving submarine. And he had wondered when and if they would be bold enough to use that lead, to step out in front of the navies of the world in a single moment.

Now they apparently had.

Eventually Volynsky ran out of things to say, just before he ran out of breath. His massive belly was heaving like the swell of the sea, and sweat was pouring down his heavy-jowled face. Barsukov let the captain mop his face with a rumpled and dirty handkerchief. Then he said, "Exactly how superior is *Devilfish* to our latest nuclear submarines?"

Volynsky frowned. "Exact figures are—"

"All right then—approximately! And be quick! I

45

don't have all day, Comrade Captain. The next time you give a report perhaps you had better remember that!"

Volynsky looked sulky but replied quickly. "She can dive at least twice as deep, travel at least one-third faster, and carries more advanced electronics equipment."

The last went without saying, Barsukov realized. American electronics were at least five years—one, perhaps two generations—ahead of Soviet. Perhaps the gap might be closed before he died, but he didn't have many hopes. In any case, that was one more thing that couldn't be helped for now.

He realized that he was sitting and staring at Volynsky in silence and that the fat man was beginning to fidget. The admiral continued to stare in silence for a minute longer, until sweat was breaking out on Volynsky's face. Then he rose.

"Thank you, Comrade Captain. You have been most informative. I think we can put your information to good use."

Volynsky correctly took Barsukov's words as dismissal. He heaved himself up out of his chair, stood at something like attention, saluted sloppily, and went out.

When the door had closed behind Volynsky, Barsukov sat back down at his desk, picked up a pencil, and began jotting down notes on the back of an old envelope.

First. Request another probe of this "Office of Special Submarine Operations" that seemed to control *Devilfish*, whatever it was. Find out who was running it, what their reputations were, what they might be expected to do. Find out the performance of the men. Volynsky was a fool if he thought that only the performance of the submarine made any difference. He probably was a fool, in that area. He had never been to sea or been involved in combat. Barsukov had done both. And so he knew that a ship was no better than the men who sent her out—and even more, no better than the men aboard her.

That was something he would have to leave to the KGB, though. They had the skills and also the men on the spot. And they didn't like him looking over their shoulders any more than he liked them looking over his. In fact, it was dangerous to try to push the secret police along faster than they were willing to go. If you got too curious, you might make *them* curious. And making the KGB curious about you was a sure road to ruin.

Second. Get the best submarine in the Soviet fleet to sea with orders to find *Devilfish*, or at least look for her. The Atlantic is a big ocean, of course. But *Devilfish* seemed to be operating out of Norfolk. That gave at least a starting point. After that, the submarine could cruise until she either found *Devilfish* or reached the end of her endurance.

If *Devilfish* were found—what then? To start with, find out just exactly what she can do. Push her to the limits of her performance, if possible. Find out if she really is a super-submarine, or if Volynsky is getting nervous.

And then?

*Devilfish* might be a one-shot model. On the other hand, she might be the prototype for a whole fleet of American super-submarines that could sweep the Soviet Navy away like sharks gobbling up herring. But if she were to disappear mysteriously—well, the Americans had politicians to worry about. Their politicians were not happy to have the military's expensive toys vanish. They might get so unhappy that they would cancel the project that had produced *Devilfish*. And then there would be no fleet of super-submarines.

And if *Devilfish* could be captured? Now there was a mouth-watering and delightful thought. So delightful, in fact, that Barsukov decided to have a drink to celebrate.

He pulled a bottle of vodka out of one desk drawer, twisted the top off with his steel claw, and poured a healthy shot into a glass. As he drank it off, a silent toast popped into his mind.

"To an early victory over *Devilfish!*"

# 7

Cheever strode across the long gangplank. Behind him came a sailor, carrying Cheever's two seabags. He preferred the old-fashioned bags to suitcases—they looked more like they belonged aboard a ship, and they didn't take up much space after they were empty. That was important aboard any ship, and doubly important aboard a submarine, even one as roomy as *Devilfish.* *Devilfish's* sixty men had as much room to themselves as ninety or a hundred did aboard a regular nuclear attack submarine. But somehow gear always expanded to fill all the available space and one compartment more.

Cheever stepped down off the swaying gangplank and carefully made his way to the main access hatch in the sail. All that showed of *Devilfish* above water was her high, thin sail, part of her rudder, and the upper portion of her cigar-shaped central hull. When she was in the water, her great wings were completely submerged, and it was almost impossible to distinguish her from a standard submarine. That hadn't been planned by her designers; it was pure luck. Very good luck, too, thought Cheever. Otherwise *Devilfish* would be instantly recognizable to any casual yachtsman—or passing foreign agent.

The access door in the sail was closed. Good. Frank Bronson wasn't taking any chances. He was keeping *Devilfish* sealed up whenever possible, even when there was nobody around but Navy personnel and the few civilian members of the night shift.

The sail was free-flooding—it filled with water when *Devilfish* submerged. The real solid barrier between *Devilfish* and the outside world was the main hatch at Cheever's feet. The hatch itself was a tapered plug of fiberglass nearly six inches thick, swinging down into a circular, trunked hole a yard across. Massive metal dogs and latches as well as its own shape held it in place. It could resist the same pressures as the rest of *Devilfish*—better than two and a half tons per square inch. But it swung easily on its oiled hinges as Cheever lifted it without even breathing hard.

That was another of the hundreds of miracles aboard *Devilfish*. A metal hatch of that size and strength would have weighed half a ton. It would have had to be swung by an electric motor—more weight, more power consumption, more machinery to maintain and repair. And suppose the motor went out? It would be hard for enough men to get close to the hatch to lift it. Redundancy—having three or four ways of doing everything essential—was a basic principle of sound engineering. *Devilfish* had it as no other submarine had ever had it before.

The hatch swung lightly open and Cheever climbed down the ladder into the conning tower. The hatch clicked shut behind the sailor with the bags. Cheever climbed on down into the control room. It was deserted except for a sonarman 2/c who had his head

49

and torso buried beneath a console. There was an electronics testing pack on the desk beside him.

Cheever went forward, into the wardroom, and found Frank Bronson sitting at the gray and green table, sipping coffee. The executive officer stood up as Cheever entered.

"Welcome back, sir."

"Thanks, Frank." Cheever flicked his eyes farther aft, toward the small blue door with the sign "Commanding Officer" on it. Bronson nodded and followed his captain.

Cheever's cabin was roomy for a submarine. It was very nearly seven feet wide, with a bed, three lockers, a washbasin, desk, and chair—all of them folding. Standing in the middle of it with his arms stretched out, Cheever (who was just over six feet tall) could not touch the walls. That made the cabin practically ballroom-sized by submarine standards.

Bronson sat down on the bed while Cheever pulled out the folding chair and squatted on it.

"Well, Frank?"

"One problem, sir. Rabinowitz has gone to the hospital with appendicitis."

Cheever frowned. Even in a crew of experts and specialists, Quartermaster 1/c Marcus Rabinowitz was a hard man to lose, however temporarily. He was one of the assigned operators for the Mark II deep diver, the high-performance minisub that *Devilfish* carried in a bay just forward of her reactor compartment. With Rabinowitz out, they had only two qualified deep diver operators aboard—Fishman Nielsen and Bronson himself. That could be awkward if they had to make extensive use of the minisub.

"Any chance of getting a replacement before we sail?"

Bronson shook his head. "I already shot a request straight up to Cappel himself. Not a chance."

"Oh, well, if it can't be helped—" Cheever sighed. "How are things otherwise?"

"Four-oh, sir." Bronson grinned. "The four techs for the processor are all bunked down in number seven berthing compartment. They don't look too happy, but they didn't expect to be. They'll manage."

"Good. What about McNeil?"

"He's not on board yet, that I've heard."

Again Cheever couldn't help frowning. McNeil wasn't going to get off on the right foot aboard *Devilfish* if they had to delay sailing for him. He looked at his watch. It was 2100. They were supposed to cast off at 2130.

Bronson noticed Cheever's concern. "Don't worry about it, sir. The processor's purring like a kitten. No problems there."

"All right." Cheever stood up, remembering to duck his head slightly to keep from banging it against a pipe that ran directly over the seat. "I'm going up to the control room." He reached into the breast pocket of his coat and handed Bronson an envelope. "Our orders for the voyage. Cappel specifically told me to have you read them before we cast off. Just in case."

Cheever went out of the cabin and into the wardroom. He sat down at the head of the table.

"Steward?"

Chief Steward Perez stuck his head out of the galley. "Sir?"

"Coffee."

"Aye aye, sir. Want a doughnut? The cook just ran up a fresh batch."

Cheever's mouth watered at the thought of one of Mike O'Hara's piping-hot doughnuts, but he knew he had to rein in his sweet tooth while *Devilfish* was at sea and exercise opportunities were limited. Ashore he could work off the extra calories playing tennis, swimming, or sailing. But aboard *Devilfish* he had to watch

51

himself. Otherwise, he might put ten pounds on his lean frame before he could turn around.

He shook his head. "Just the coffee. And black."

The coffee arrived at the same moment as Commander Lerone McNeil. Cheever rose as the big scientist entered the wardroom. They shook hands. "Welcome aboard *Devilfish*, Commander. Shall I have someone show you to your cabin?"

"Someone already did," said McNeil, with a wry grin. "I've seen larger telephone booths. But I travel light. No problem."

"Good. The executive officer says the processor is running perfectly, but I imagine you'd like to check it out."

"I certainly would, Captain. Which way?"

Cheever pointed aft. The scientist disappeared down the passageway at a trot. Cheever suddenly remembered a junction box in the overhead halfway down the passageway that might hang low enough for somebody the size of McNeil to—

He sprang to his feet. "Doctor, watch out for—"

"Ouch! Goddamn!" came floating back down the passageway.

"Are you all right, Commander?"

"I guess so." There was the sound of a door closed hard—almost slammed—as McNeil passed on to the next compartment.

Cheever sighed. McNeil obviously wasn't going to feel particularly at home aboard *Devilfish*. But then submarines weren't a natural or congenial environment for most people. As long as McNeil kept his head and did his work, there wouldn't be any problems.

He stood up. Time to go up onto the bridge and start getting ready. He looked at his watch. 2110. Twenty minutes to go.

Cheever looked fore and aft along *Devilfish*'s sleek

52

blackness. The bridge loudspeaker fizzed and crackled, then said, "Engine room to bridge. Ready on both engines."

"Prepare to back dead slow on both. Mark!"

A faint vibration crept through *Devilfish*. Cheever looked aft. Two patches of water were slowly churning themselves into foam as *Devilfish's* two six-bladed propellers dug in. Then Cheever looked forward.

"Cast off bow spring."

The dockyard men hurried to lift the looped end of the wire hawser from the heavy steel bollard. It splashed into the water of the drydock as the powered winch recessed in *Devilfish's* bow wound it in. The last of the hawser vanished and the two sailors standing on the main deck by the winch slammed the cover down on it.

Now *Devilfish's* last tie to the land was broken. Cheever pressed the loudspeaker button.

"Secure mooring party. Clear the main deck." The two sailors unhooked their safety lines and scuttled aft to the main access door in the sail. They vanished below like rabbits down a rabbit hole. *Devilfish's* main deck was rounded and slick and could easily be treacherous. Except for mooring and unmooring, it was rare for anybody to have any reason to be on it.

*Devilfish's* stern was emerging from under the roof of the drydock. Slowly she crept out into Hampton Roads. As the bow slid out into the open, Cheever looked up at the sky. The wind was light, not more than ten miles an hour, and the sky largely clear. When they were out and away from the glaring lights of the city, they should be able to see the stars. Cheever knew that it was an odd belief of his, perhaps pure superstition. But somehow he always felt better if he could get one last look at the sun or the stars before taking a submarine down for a long submerged voyage.

No time for that now, though. *Devilfish* was now

53

well out into Hampton Roads, with plenty of room to turn.

"Ahead one-third on port, back one-third on starboard."

The vibration became stronger and oddly irregular. *Devilfish* began to swing around. With one of her propellers going ahead and the other astern, *Devilfish* had a turning radius that had to be seen and experienced to be believed. She could, quite literally, run circles around any other submarine in existence.

In minutes *Devilfish* had come about, and her blunt bow was pointing downriver. The Norfolk-Newport News bridge arched across the darkness, the cars crossing it visible as fast-moving sparks of light.

"Ahead slow."

The vibration faded and settled down as *Devilfish*'s propellers began to turn together, pushing her ahead down Hampton Roads. She slid under the bridge at a sedate ten knots. That was a sluggish crawl for her, but it was the only safe speed in the crowded harbor.

A cabin cruiser with less concern for safety overtook *Devilfish*, racing past her at twice her speed.

"Tourists," said a disgusted voice beside Cheever. He turned to see Bronson standing beside him.

"How's it going, Frank?"

"No problems, as usual. McNeil's locked himself in with the processor. I think he's going to be watching over that machine like a mother hen with one chick all the way out and all the way back."

"I don't blame him. It's his baby. He's got a lot more riding on its success than we do, even with Senator Bergen and the rest."

"It's nice to be getting back to sea again, sir. Where we don't have to worry about people like Bergen."

Cheever nodded. The two officers stood side by side on the bridge, guiding *Devilfish* through the traffic-clogged waters. There was silence except for Cheever's occasional orders and the acknowledgments from the helmsman in the control room below.

They passed under the Chesapeake Bay Bridge. The girders of the huge suspension span loomed high above them, then drifted away astern. When the bridge had faded to a dim bulk silhouetted against the distant glow of the city's lights, Cheever swung his eyes in a complete circle around *Devilfish*. He looked at the radar repeater in its recessed console. Neither his eyes nor the ship's surface-warning radar showed any other ships in a position to be dangerous.

"All ahead, full surface cruise."

*Devilfish* seemed to leap ahead like a drag racer heading down the quarter-mile. Actually, she was only increasing her speed to twenty knots or so. Like all nuclear submarines, she was a creature of the deeps. On the surface she was as ugly, clumsy, and vulnerable as a coal barge. She became completely uncontrollable on the surface at much over twenty knots. Even at twenty knots, she had an unpredictable tendency to dig her blunt snout in deep and give the bridge watch an unexpected soaking.

But tonight the sea was almost as calm as a river, with a long, gentle swell that gave *Devilfish* hardly any motion that Cheever could detect. He stayed on the bridge while Bronson went below to make one final inspection. Perez sent up more coffee. This time he also sent up the doughnuts—chocolate-covered and still warm—and Cheever did not turn them down. He munched while he listened to the reports from the control room.

"Course one-two-oh. Speed nineteen. Depth sixteen fathoms."

Cheever heard that report seven times. The first two phrases were always the same. But gradually the water deepened. There were eighteen fathoms under *Devilfish*'s keel.

55

Then twenty-one.

Twenty-four.

Twenty-nine.

Cheever made up his mind to dive when the depth report was forty fathoms.

Thirty-six.

The bottom was dropping off faster now. Next time—

"Course one-two-oh. Speed nineteen. Depth forty-two fathoms."

Cheever let out breath he had not realized he had been holding. Then a smile spread across his face, and he pressed the button on the intercom and gave two orders. Two orders that loomed large on any list of his dozen favorite orders. His, or any submariner's.

"Clear the bridge. Sound the diving alarm."


8


Frank Bronson, who had just poked his head up through the hatch, pulled it back down again. The two lookouts vanished after him. As Cheever stepped to the edge of the hatch, the diving alarm sounded, harsh and raucous and unmistakable.

"*Ah-goooo-ah—ah-goooo-ah!*"

*Devilfish* might have all the marvels of modern naval engineering and science aboard her and be one herself, but she still had a diving alarm that sounded like a heavy truck horn with a bad cold.

Cheever swung himself down through the hatch, pulled it shut, then scrambled down the ladder inside the sail to the main access hatch in the pressure hull. As he descended, he made a quick visual check of the gear inside the sail—the heavy vertical steel tubes that housed the periscopes and radar and the horizontal tubes for the surface-launched missiles.

Submarines had not fought on the surface regularly since World War II. And, like any nuclear submarine, *Devilfish* was ten times more lethal underwater than she could ever be on the surface. But unlike previous nuclear submarines, she was far from helpless on the surface either.

Four heavy missile-launching tubes were mounted aiming outward on either side of her sail. They could carry either cruise missiles to strike at enemy warships and merchant vessels or homing antiaircraft missiles to discourage enemy patrol planes and helicopters. *Devilfish's* best method of defense against planes and ships would always be to go deep fast. But if there was no time or no chance for that, she had a second line of defense to fall back on.

The access hatch closed behind Cheever. He made sure to turn the locking wheel until the latch indicators flipped up into the "Secure" position. Then he dropped down into the conning tower and from there into the control room.

Frank Bronson was already standing behind the officer of the watch in his chair. A glance around the control room showed everyone else in position. The chief of the watch was scanning the diving board, watching the indicators for hull openings to click into the "Closed" position.

When the last one had done so, he turned to Bronson and Cheever.

"Straight board, sir."

Cheever nodded in acknowledgment. By tem-

57

perament a man of few words, he became even more close-mouthed when it was time to take a submarine down into the sea.

"Flood main ballast. Five-degree down angle on the planes."

"Aye aye, sir."

The chief of the watch moved swiftly, opening vent switches. A faint rumble and shudder went through the ship as air spewed up from the main ballast tank, letting seawater in from below. Suddenly there was a heavy sluggishness in *Devilfish* that had not been there before. In thirty seconds her displacement shot from three thousand to three thousand five hundred tons and went on increasing.

Then it was the turn of the planesman of the watch. His hands moved, slowly and carefully, inching the control wheel around to the proper down-angle. The inclinometer on the board quivered around to four, four and a half, then five degrees down. The depth gauge began to move. Thirty feet and the hull was under, fifty feet and the last of the sail was submerged, sixty feet and the periscopes would have been vanishing if they had been raised. Eighty feet—

"Keep her going until we reach one hundred fifty," said Cheever quietly.

"Aye aye, sir."

Cheever felt uncomfortable with much less than four hundred feet of water between *Devilfish* and the surface. But when there wasn't four hundred feet of water between the surface of the sea and the hard bottom, there was nothing he could do.

A minute later the depth gauge reached a hundred and fifty feet. Without waiting for orders, the planesman moved the wheel back. Cheever felt the submarine's deck level out under his feet, and he relaxed slightly. As fantastically maneuverable as *Devilfish* was, any dive in comparatively shallow water was tricky.

And it could become dangerous very fast if anything went wrong—much faster than was possible in a dive with a mile of water under *Devilfish's* keel.

That was in startling contrast to conventional submarines, Cheever realized with a certain amusement. When one of *them* went deep, it was always nice to know that the depth of the bottom was less than your collapse depth. If anything went wrong, there was always the hope of settling into the ooze of the bottom, calling the rescue teams, and waiting for a Deep Submergence Rescue Vehicle to show up.

But *Devilfish's* collapse depth was greater than the average depth of the oceans—nearly three miles. For her, shallow water offered only the endless danger of smashing at high speed into something solid. Her massive fiberglass hull could stand it, but what about the men and gear inside? Cheever hoped he would never have to find out.

All this reminded him that it was time to set speed. He looked at the officer of the watch.

"Lieutenant Doubleday, all ahead one-third."

One-third power on both propellers would keep *Devilfish* sliding along at about the same twenty knots she had been making on the surface. That was as much as Cheever cared to try here on the continental shelf. Deep water was several hours away yet.

He decided to go aft to the experimental module compartment and see *Devilfish's* two most important passengers—the processor and its inventor.

The processor was not actually purring when Cheever entered the compartment. In fact, it was just sitting on its welded-steel base, not making a sound. Not even a hum or a gurgle. McNeil and one of his assistants were standing by the control panel in their shirt sleeves, watching the dials intently.

For a moment Cheever had a chill feeling that

something had gone spectacularly wrong with the processor before they were even well started on the Endless Voyage. Then McNeil turned to Cheever with a grin.

"She'll do nicely at a hundred psi less than we thought she could."

Cheever managed to keep a blank expression off his face, but McNeil detected his confusion and filled him in. Not parading his knowledge, Cheever noted. And he also noted with approval McNeil's shirt sleeves. Being able to get in there and work alongside one's men was an important part of Cheever's notion of a leader. Young officers who came to him with qualms about getting their hands dirty either shaped up or shipped out very soon.

Either McNeil was very much on his good behavior, or he was feeling better and more relaxed. Cheever hoped it was the second alternative. But he'd take the first if he had to.

"The catalytic reaction operates best at very high pressures and temperatures—at least two-thousand psi and six-hundred degrees," said McNeil. "But we're not getting any major raw material inputs right now. And we won't be until we're several days farther out."

Cheever nodded. "Meanwhile, we can all eat the steak and turkey the supply officer laid in."

McNeil laughed. "I suppose so. But anyway—the reaction has to be maintained, or we have the problem of starting it up again. That takes time and work and it stresses the machinery a lot more than regular operation, because of the fluctuating pressures. They set up vibration patterns and can lead to the shearing of key fittings. That wouldn't be good."

That was a considerable understatement. Having *anything* at 2000 psi and 600 degrees spewing into a compartment aboard *Devilfish* was a nasty prospect.

"Don't worry, Captain," said McNeil. Cheever noted that the scientist was calling him by his title rather than his rank. That was correct usage, now that they were at sea. Score another point for McNeil. "That's why we're trying to find the lowest pressure and temperature where we can keep the reaction going. So far we've got it down to under half normal operating pressures."

"Good," said Cheever. He didn't feel that he had the technical expertise or any particular reason to make a longer remark. Everything seemed to be in order here—including Doctor McNeil's frame of mind.

As Cheever headed forward, the bosun's pipe signaled an announcement over the PA system.

"Now hear this. Now hear this. Breakfast will be served in the crew's mess hall starting in ten minutes. Breakfast will be served in the crew's mess hall starting in ten minutes. The smoking lamp is lit in all authorized spaces."

Cheever looked at his watch. It was almost 0400 and he had been awake for nearly thirty hours, on his feet most of the time. He was not yet really tired, but he knew that he would be if he didn't get some sleep fairly soon. And that would be breaking one of his personal rules—never let an emergency catch you tired or hungry if you can possibly avoid it.

He headed for his cabin. Inside, he pressed the button on the intercom and spoke to the officer of the watch.

"This is the captain. I'm going to turn in for a few hours. If we cross the continental shelf before I'm up, wait until the depth is a thousand feet. Then take her down to six hundred and increase speed to thirty knots."

"Aye aye, sir."

Cheever stuffed his clothes into the locker, wrestled the door shut, and climbed into the narrow bed. Deliberately blanking any possible worries out of his mind, he let himself drift slowly off to sleep.

Three hours later, while her captain slept, *Devilfish* reached the drop-off. The officer of the watch saw the fathometer plunge downward. Its needle reached a thousand feet and kept dropping.

"Five degrees down-angle," he said to the planesman of the watch. "Six hundred feet." And to the engine room, "Make revolutions for thirty knots."

*Devilfish* raced out into the deep Atlantic, sliding through the water at a steadily increasing speed.

9

Admiral Barsukov sat in his office in Murmansk and looked at the small man on the other side of the desk. The office and the desk were also small, so Barsukov could see the man clearly. He could see every line in the man's hard face, the gray in his temples and in his bushy eyebrows, the sharp-pointed, deeply cleft chin, the immaculate uniform with the commander's bars on the shoulders of the coat. The commander's name was Semyon Lukin, and his ship was the atomic submarine *Thunderbolt*.

It was pure coincidence that Lukin was commanding a ship with that name at this time. It was almost certain that he would be commanding one of the largest Soviet nuclear submarines. Barsukov was not the only high official in the Soviet Navy with a high opinion of Commander Lukin. But if Lukin had by some ill chance been commanding a garbage scow in Vladivostok, Barsukov would still have snatched him up and put him aboard a submarine.

Coincidence. But a happy one. Barsukov was too good a Communist to permit himself to openly believe in superstitious nonsense like good or bad omens, but he could not help feeling good about the name. He was about to throw Lukin and his ship like a thunderbolt at *Devilfish.*

He realized that he had been silent for so long that Lukin was beginning to fidget. And he could not explain why he had been silent. The little commander was as hard and grim and humorless as the stainless steel of the pressure vessel of *Thunderbolt's* own reactor. If he had ever been able to appreciate the kind of notion that was running through Admiral Barsukov's mind, it had been many years ago.

"To continue," said Barsukov, making his voice deliberately more harsh than usual, "an illegal operation has been requested to increase our knowledge of *Devilfish* and her capabilities. The organs of state security appreciate our need and the importance of *Devilfish,* so I think the mission will be executed. Any information it produces will of course be passed on to you as soon as possible."

Lukin nodded without speaking. He was not much more talkative than something made of steel, either.

Barsukov stubbed out a dying cigarette stub with his claw-hand. "We can be sure that *Devilfish* is superior to any submarine we have. Don't allow yourself any illusions on the subject. The writers for *Red Fleet* magazine who say we have the best of everything don't have to take ships out to sea against the Americans."

Again Lukin's only response was a nod.

"In particular, their superiority in electronics is recognized by everyone who—who has had to deal with it in the field." He had nearly said, "who has enough brains to find the john when he wants to go." But even "secure" offices like this one had been known to sprout ears on very short notice. Barsukov did not want to endanger himself or the mission by expressing his true opinion too often or too loudly where those ears might hear.

"If *Devilfish* is an experimental model, she may well have been fitted with electronics a full additional generation in advance of anything we've met with so far. Assume you'll be detected by the Americans well before you detect them.

"The question is, though, how long before? *Devilfish* may be able to run circles around *Thunderbolt*. Force her to do just that, watch her as she runs, and bring back what you see. That's what we need more than anything else, so it has first priority."

Lukin nodded, but this time he also spoke. "What about extraordinary measures?" In other words—what about trying to capture or destroy *Devilfish?*

Barsukov couldn't help hesitating for a moment while he thought out the best words for his answer. The chair-warmers in Moscow wouldn't like what he was going to say, if they ever heard of it. Some of them perhaps really believed in that stupid "detente" with the West. All of them at least had to talk and act as if they believed it.

Then Barsukov grinned and relaxed. If Moscow ever heard what he was going to say, it would only be through the secret police. And he couldn't imagine the secret police wanting to get somebody in trouble for playing rough with the Americans! The idea almost made him laugh.

Then he went on briskly. "You will have a team of four picked sabotage divers aboard, plus demolition charges, gas, and the rest." He looked at his watch. "They should be going aboard *Thunderbolt* now. And you can use the PKG prefix for any operational signals connected with the capture or destruction of *Devil-fish.*"

It was Lukin's turn to smile as thinly as he always did. The PKG prefix was the special one that a Soviet submarine could use to call on any Soviet ship in her area for assistance—warships, merchant vessels, the far-flung fishing fleet with its spy trawlers and oceanographic research vessels. The resources that the Soviet Union could bring to aid its submarines in distant seas were not yet equal to those of the Americans. But they were not to be ignored, and they were growing every month. If they could make it possible to capture *Devilfish* and bring her treasure-house of innovations home to the Soviet Union—

"Use your discretion," he said to Lukin. "The secret of getting the most out of such a capture is keeping it unknown to the enemy. That was why the Americans did so well with the German submarine they captured in the Fatherland War, the U-505. They kept the capture secret until the war was over and it was too late for the Germans to get any benefit out of it."

"I understand. If there is any danger that a capture might be detected—" Lukin let his sentence trail off meaningfully, rather than ask a direct question.

"The same rules apply to destruction," Barsukov said quickly. "Destroying an enemy warship on the high seas in peacetime is an act of war. But we've managed it before. If you can manage it again—well, *Devilfish* must be very expensive. And the American politicians are easy to scare when their expensive military equipment vanishes. Mysteriously, Lukin. *Mysteriously.* If it can be done that way—it is up to you and your crew. But make all your reports first."

There was no need for Barsukov to explain that last warning. Lukin was as farmiliar as anyone and more so than most with the deadly games that submarines could play in the deep seas—games that could suddenly explode into something more than games. Then thunder would roll through the seas, swiftly followed by silence. Where there had been two submarines, there would be only one, plus some oil and debris drifting up from far below.

Sometimes there would be no submarines. A submarine could fire a homing torpedo or a nuclear-armed rocket in the last seconds before her own death. Then the victor would also die, before her crew had even had a chance to enjoy their victory.

Barsukov had sent many men to their deaths and would go on doing it. He would go on doing it with no qualms or strain, either. Weak men should not serve the Soviet Union. But neither would he ever blind himself to the dangers he was asking others to run. Day-to-day living in the Soviet Union involved too much lying already. Here was one place where he did not even have to lie to himself, let alone to others.

Lukin's nod this time was a bare jerk of the head to show that he understood. Then he rose and picked up his hat from the arm of his chair.

"With your permission, Comrade Admiral—?"

"Of course." Barsukov rose to his feet. The two officers exchanged salutes and Lukin went out. It seemed to Barsukov that the closing of the door behind the little commander echoed through the office like the explosion of a depth charge.

The sun was just slipping below the horizon when Barsukov's helicopter landed him on the little cape. He climbed out, holding his hat on his head against the rotor wash. Then he walked slowly by himself to the very edge of the drop down into the sea and looked out over the water.

There she came, right on schedule like the Moscow subway. Lukin was like that. The long, low, black hull came sliding along, ploughing a white-foamed furrow through the silver-gray water. Lukin had *Thunderbolt* driving along at her maximum surface speed, and her bow wave rose up over her blunt stem and threw spray over her bridge. The lookouts would be getting wet. So would Lukin. But the little man wouldn't be bothered. He never was.

Barsukov watched the small figures on *Thunderbolt's* bridge until he could no longer distinguish them. He went on watching the long black shape race away across the sea until it too was almost impossible to make out in the deepening twilight. Then he walked back to his helicopter. Things were off to a good start.

The hunt was on.


# 10


Admiral Cappel's secretary brought him a yellow message flimsy. He read it and snorted with satisfaction.

*Devilfish* was a thousand miles out into the Atlantic on her Endless Voyage. All systems functioning normally, including the processor. It hadn't produced any food yet, but it hadn't given any trouble. Neither had Doctor McNeil. No unusual conditions to report. The submarine was maintaining thirty knots and a depth of six hundred feet.

That was wise of Cheever. *Devilfish* offered any competent and aggressive CO almost unlimited opportunities for showing off. If anybody happened to be around to watch while *Devilfish* was performing to her incredible limits, they might see some interesting sights that it was much better they shouldn't see.

Cheever knew that. So *Devilfish* was moving out into the Atlantic at a speed and depth any modern nuclear attack submarine could easily match. No inquisitive sonar could pick out an echo barreling along at twice the speed of any ordinary submarine.

And both McNeil and the processor were behaving themselves. That was also good news. Cappel hadn't been much worried about the processor. McNeil seldom had a hand in anything that didn't work. The man was a genius, but Cappel had to agree with Cheever that he could also be hard to handle every so often. And a submerged submarine on a long voyage wasn't the best place for somebody like that—if there was any choice in the matter. However, there wasn't.

The next thing his secretary brought Cappel was the morning's *Washington Post*. The WAVE's expression told the admiral even before he opened the paper that it held bad news. After he read the article she pointed out, his own expression became just as unhappy.

The headline read:

## BERGEN FLAYS SECRET INTELLIGENCE OPERATIONS

### Calls for Abolition of "Gateways to Fascism"

Underneath the headline was a double-column picture of Senator Bergen. In profile, as usual. In profile he looked remarkably like a younger and smoother-featured Abraham Lincoln. He knew it, and he could usually rely on having at least one news photographer around who knew it too and who could be trusted to catch the right angle. The man had no trouble looking sincere, at any rate. His big problem was not looking like a backwoods farmboy.

However, Cappel didn't give a damn one way or the other what Bergen looked like. If he would just stop running off at the mouth concerning things he didn't know anything about, he could turn purple and go bald for all Cappel cared. But if the article had him quoted correctly, he was obviously planning to go on to bigger and better things.

He had addressed a rally of something called the United Political Action Council in San Francisco. He had called for the "immediate abolition of all clandestine intelligence agencies and activities—these gateways to Fascism for our free country."

That by itself was enough to annoy Cappel. He didn't give the intelligence agencies his blessing all the time, since he wasn't an idiot. But he had been around too long and seen too much of the real world to follow Bergen's notions. The intelligence agencies, as far as he was concerned, were more like sentries at the gates. Sometimes they let slip in what should have been kept out. More often they kept out (and annoyed and spied on) what they could have safely let in. But they did a pretty good job most of the time. What more could a reasonable man expect?

The problem was that Bergen didn't seem to be reasonable. Neither did the people he had been talking to. They had cheered every new slap at the agencies, including his list of the ones he proposed to abolish. It started with the Central Intelligence Agency and worked down the alphabet soup of initials to some that even Cappel had barely heard of. On the way down, the list included the Office of Special Submarine Operations.

Cappel swore long and loud. He used every word he had picked up since he was six years old. Then he stood up, threw the newspaper into the wastebasket, and buzzed for the secretary.

He didn't much care whether Bergen was reasonable or not. And he didn't much care about regulations, which frowned on what he was about to do. He was going down to see Bergen and try to talk some sense into the man. He didn't have much hope, but what the hell! —what was there to lose? If nothing else, he could size him up better face-to-face than by reading about him in the papers.

"Senator Bergen will see you now, Mr. Cappel," said the young man behind the big desk. The sign on it read "Charles Pender, Administrative Assistant." He looked rather like a junior faculty member at some small college—intelligent, but not very vigorous.

Pender certainly could use a lesson in official courtesy, Cappel thought. He had at least a courtesy right to the title of "Admiral" and most people had the sense or good manners to use it. At least the ones who wanted to make a good impression. Pender obviously didn't give a damn about helping the admiral's meeting with his boss get off to a good start. Cappel wondered if Pender also reflected that boss's attitude. If he did, this meeting was probably going to be a complete waste of time.

Bergen at least stood up when Cappel entered and held out a bony hand.

"Good afternoon, Admiral Cappel. Very glad you could drop in. What did you want to discuss?"

Cappel fought down an urge to reply, "You know perfectly well, Senator." Snappy comebacks weren't going to help matters at all.

"I wanted to discuss your charges against some of the intelligence agencies, Senator. I—"

"That involves discussion of classified matter, Admiral. Can I be sure of your security clearance?"

70

Cappel counted to ten, nearly doing it out loud. Then he said evenly, "Senator Bergen. If you want to waste your time and mine, you can doubt my security clearance. You can call up the Atomic Energy Commission, the Chief of Naval Operations, Admiral Rickover, or quite a few other people. They'll all tell you that I have Q clearance. Security clearances don't get any higher than that, Senator."

Bergan nodded. "I know that, Admiral. I also know that the military-bureaucratic alliance covers each other's stories very carefully. Particularly when it's a matter of supporting some unpopular lobbying effort."

This time Cappel counted to twenty. "Senator, you used the word 'lobbying.' I didn't. You haven't let me say a word on what I came here for. And you're coming perilously close to calling me a liar, which I—don't think will do us much good." He could have finished the sentence much more forcefully than that, and nearly did. But he decided to give the Senator one more chance.

Bergen took it. "All right, Admiral. I apologize. I didn't intend to imply that either you or any of the other distinguished public servants and institutions you mentioned would lie on a matter this important." He rummaged a cigarette box out of his desk. "Would you like a cigarette? I don't smoke myself, but—"

Cappel shook his head. He knew perfectly well that Senator Bergen didn't smoke. It was part of his image as the natural-food man, filled with organic vitamins. He also didn't want to let Bergen give him anything before he had said his piece, even a cigarette. That would be bad negotiating tactics.

Cappel settled back in his chair. He knew this gave an impression of rocklike solidity that disconcerted a good many people. The idea of asking him to leave didn't even occur to those people. Then he grinned.

"Senator, I head the Office of Special Submarine

Operations. That's one of the agencies you want to sweep away. I'm not going to argue the pros and cons of the other agencies with you. I don't know much more about their activities than I read in the papers. Probably less than you do, in fact." That was a good negotiating tactic—admitting one weakness. Only one, and of course the other person doesn't know what an irrelevant weakness it is. But it makes him think you're less formidable than you are. Over-confidence is an occupational disease of politicians, anyway.

"However, O.S.S.O. is my baby. I didn't quite think it up all by myself, but I've headed it since it was just a file in the CNO's office. I know what it does, and what it doesn't do. One of the things it doesn't do is clandestine intelligence work, the kind you're worried about."

Senator Bergen's face hardened. "Admiral, I can't honestly imagine that you expect me to believe that." As Cappel's face also froze, he added hastily, "At least not on your word alone. I won't mince words—there have been too many denials of such operations that were flat-out lies. Some of those lies have come from high officers of the United States Navy, Admiral. So if all I can get is your personal assurances, I can't accept them as sufficient. Even if I wanted to, my colleagues in the proposed Intelligence Operations Committee probably wouldn't."

Bergen paused, which was fortunate. It gave Cappel time to make quite sure he wasn't going to lose his temper. It also let him realize that Bergen was up to something. The admiral made himself look as much like the Rock of Gibraltar as possible. Then he waited for Bergen's counterproposal.

The Senator cleared his throat. "However, I'm always willing to be convinced, at least on a case-by-case basis. If I and one or two of my personal staff could tour your installations and examine a reasonable selection of files, I think—" His voice trailed into silence as he saw Cappel's face set into the hardest mold yet.

Behind that mold Cappel was thinking furiously. It was a tempting offer, and one obviously designed to be tempting. Throw O.S.S.O. open to Senator Bergen's curiosity, and he would ensure *Devilfish* a future. No, he might give *Devilfish* a future. He might also give her an even swifter end.

O.S.S.O. would be completely at the mercy of how Bergen decided to use what he learned. Possibly he would be impressed and would keep his mouth shut. But it was more likely that he would misinterpret something he saw or read, jump to conclusions, and spread the word all over the headlines—*BERGEN EXPOSES SUBVERSIVE SUB AGENCY.*

It was also possible that he would simply spout off boastfully about how much O.S.S.O. trusted him. To prove how much they trusted him, he could easily wind up revealing much that should be kept secret. Bergen had presidential ambitions, or so the Washington scuttlebutt ran. Politicians with presidential ambitions often weren't too careful about what they said if they thought it would help them.

Besides, there were practical problems. Senator Bergen wanted to take a tour of O.S.S.O.'s installations. How the hell could he, when the most important installation of all was a thousand miles out in the Atlantic? No, probably closer to fifteen hundred now.

Cappel shook his head. "That probably wouldn't be practical, Senator." He used the word "probably" to soften the refusal, although he wasn't feeling very soft toward the man on the other side of the big walnut desk. He added, "Unless you and your staff were willing to agree to keep everything you saw, read, or heard entirely secret."

Bergen frowned. "Admiral, that is a request I wish you hadn't made. You are implying that my staff and I should close our eyes to any illegal operations by your department. That would be a violation of my oath of office and of my duty as a representative of the American people. And it would be a violation of the principle of the supremacy of the civil over the military in our government. You are essentially asking that I promise to assist in any cover-up of illegal operations against the interests of the American people. I will not, Admiral Cappel. But I will remember that you asked me."

Cappel decided there was no point in not speaking his mind now. "Senator, if you're going to make speeches instead of talking seriously, I made a mistake coming here. I think—"

"I certainly agree you made a mistake, Admiral, if you wanted to help your office. I didn't consider it a very high-priority target before. Now I'm going to make it a focal point of the Intelligence Operations Committee's investigations. You and your staff can expect to receive subpoenas from the committee before this is over, Admiral. I—yes, Charlie?"

Cappel turned around in his chair. Pender was standing in the door to the outer office. "Sorry, sir. But your appointment with Mr. Fanshawe is coming up in five minutes. I thought Mr. Cappel—"

"Admiral Cappel," the admiral corrected him.

"Sorry," Pender said. He didn't sound sorry.

Cappel rose to his feet. He did not offer to shake hands with Senator Bergen. It would have been sheer hypocrisy. But he wasn't able to resist the temptation to have the last word. The damage was done, anyway.

"Thank you for your time, Senator," he said. "When you're through playing games with the security of this country, call me again. Maybe then we can talk more usefully."

He went out, leaving Bergen sitting at his desk. Pender followed him to the door. There was an unmistakably hostile look on the young man's face, but Cappel decided to ignore it. Pender wasn't a problem.

But as for Senator Bergen— Cappel was muttering to himself as he walked out to his car. "Before this is over, I'm going to nail that son of a bitch to the wall!"

## II

There were times when Cheever thought the processor ought to bubble and boil and hiss like a leaky boiler— or maybe a witch's cauldron. Then, on the other hand, there were those pressures of 2000 psi and the temperatures of 600 degrees. If the processor ever started bubbling and hissing instead of sitting there quietly, *Devilfish* would have a major problem aboard.

McNeil and one of his assistants were moving around among the gleaming cylinders. As Cheever watched them, he realized how opinions about the processor had changed among the crew of *Devilfish*.

When they first went to sea, nobody except Cheever and Bronson had cared much one way or the other about whether the processor worked. In fact, Cheever suspected that at least half the crew wouldn't have minded if it didn't work at all. That way they wouldn't have to eat any of its products. All sorts of horrible rumors were supposed to be going around the ship about what the processor's food would look, taste, and smell like. Cheever didn't worry about those rumors. If they got out of hand, Fishman Nielsen would tell him—or do something about them without telling him.

But rumors aside, the officers and men were gradually getting interested in the processor. There was usually a handful of off-watch men standing in the door to the module compartment, craning their necks in the hope of seeing something interesting. They were always disappointed. The processor went quietly about its business with no uproar of flashing lights. The only thing moving around it was usually Doctor McNeil.

The scientist had done a good deal to "sell" the processor. In the process, he had done a good deal more to sell himself to Cheever. The scientist seemed cheerful, self-confident, relaxed. He laughed and joked with his assistants and answered even the silliest questions from the crew with complete good humor.

But of course why shouldn't McNeil be beaming like a proud father, with the processor running so smoothly and everybody's eyes on him? For the time being, he was the star of the show Devilfish was putting on. But suppose something went wrong with the processor? Or Devilfish got into a tight situation? How would McNeil show up then? Cheever decided it wasn't yet time to give the scientist a clean bill of health.

McNeil pulled his head out from underneath the processor, where he had been inspecting some obscure connection, and straightened up. He wiped his huge hands on a lab coat that had been white when the Endless Voyage began and grinned at Cheever.

"Well, Doctor, how's it going?"

"First-class," said McNeil, holding up a circle of thumb and forefinger. "As a matter of fact, I think we're going to be able to tap the food store for the first time today." He looked at his watch. "Say about 1430. Maybe you'd better pass the word on to the cook."

Cheever nodded. "Can do, Doctor." He didn't guarantee that the cook was going to be happy, however. Chief Petty Officer Mike O'Hara, the senior cook aboard *Devilfish*, had been one of the loudest skeptics about the processor. If anything went wrong, the processor was going to get at least one big, long, loud Irish horselaugh.

In summer the waters around Iceland teem with the fishing fleets of a dozen nations, starting with those of Iceland itself. The exception is the waters to the north, in the Denmark Straits. There the seas are chill, fog-ridden, ice-clogged even in summer.

There *Bismarck* and *Hood* met in 1941, and there *Hood* lies to this day with fourteen hundred men. There merchant vessels on the Russian convoys in 1942 took refuge from the Luftwaffe in the ice packs, beneath the clouds and fog. Nobody goes there unless he has to, and few people have to unless they wish to escape detection.

*Thunderbolt* and Commander Semyon Lukin wished to escape detection.

So *Thunderbolt* was racing through the dark, chill waters deep below the surface of the Denmark Straits. Her propeller tore the water, thrusting her forward at just below her maximum speed. Lukin sat in his cabin and listened to the vibrations the racing turbines sent through his ship. They were good, strong engines and she was a good, strong ship that would hold up to anything. If there was weakness aboard *Thunderbolt*, it would be in the human element, the ninety-odd officers and men of her crew. And if there was any weakness there, Lukin would deal with it ruthlessly.

He watched the sonar repeater on the bulkhead of his cabin. From two hundred meters down, the ice floes on the surface and the occasional whale were only faint, flickering lights on the dark screen. The monotonous "pinnngggg—pinnnggg—pinnngg" of the sonar beam made a steady beat in Lukin's ears.

He looked at the chart spread out on the little steel folding desk. *Thunderbolt* was forty miles off the northern coast of Iceland now. At her present speed she would be clear of Iceland in another three hours. Then she could turn south, past the west coast of Iceland, and out into the open Atlantic.

Then the search for this mysterious *Devilfish* could begin in earnest. The Atlantic was a big ocean, to be sure, and even the largest submarine a very small thing to find in it. But Lukin did not have a high opinion of the Americans' ability. Barsukov was a pessimist of the worst sort! The Americans almost always sent their submarines east along particular routes. The most important one crossed the Mid-Atlantic Ridge just south of Lubbock Seamount.

And if *Devilfish* was going south instead of east? Well, then there was another route the Americans used, nine times out of ten. To cover it, one would head for Estancia Seamount.

Admittedly, it would be better to have two submarines, one to cover each route, and perhaps a third to cover the approaches to the Caribbean. Asking one submarine to search out another in the wide Atlantic was a large order, even when the other submarine was American.

But Admiral Barsukov had asked him to do just that with *Thunderbolt*. Very good. He would do his best. But if he did not succeed after that—well, it was Admiral Barsukov who had sent out inadequate forces to accomplish this mission. Not Commander Semyon Lukin.

"Pressure seal check."

"Pressure seals holding, sir," said the technician.

McNeil nodded. "Feed pump check."

"Feed pump on standby. All components registering clear."

"Activate feed pump, 200 psi."

"Activating feed pump, sir." The technician flipped a black switch from vertical to horizontal. Instantly the processor shuddered and gave off a *blurrrrrp!* It sounded like a gigantic container of whipped cream being squirted. McNeil kept an eagle-eyed watch on the monitor dials.

"Pressure build-up in Segment 6," he said. "The pressure bleed-off valve must not be working right. Reduce feed pressure to 150 psi."

"Reducing pressure to 150 psi," said the technician. The whipped-cream noise faded away. McNeil turned to Cheever and the others watching from the forward end of the module compartment. It looked as if half the crew was there. The latecomers in the rear were craning their necks, trying to get a better view.

McNeil shook his head at all this eagerness. "There won't be anything to see for a while. We're feeding the processed food matter into the containers now. The pressure was building too high in the feed valve, so we cut it back a little. Otherwise we might have ruptured the connection with the container and had the gunk—I mean the processed food—all over the deck. Hell of a cleaning job." Some of the men laughed.

Suddenly the processor started making whipped-cream noises again, louder than before. It also began to shake like a nervous horse. Even from where he was standing, Cheever could see two lights on the monitor board turn red.

McNeil clenched his massive jaw until the muscles of his cheeks tightened into knots, but his cool head and professional training did not desert him. He promptly went over to the processor and listened until he had apparently detected the center of the trouble. Then he stepped back, pivoted on one leg, and drove his other foot hard into the side of the offending steel cylinder. The size-twelve shoe made a solid *clang* as it slammed into the metal. The processor quivered all over, hiccupped twice, and went back to working normally.

Cheever couldn't help applauding. After a few seconds the rest of the watchers joined him. McNeil turned around, bowing theatrically as the applause rose and then died away. "Gentlemen, I have just demonstrated the virtues of a technical education."

Something went *beeeeep* on the monitor board. McNeil looked at it, then grinned. "I think you are also about to see the first container come off the processor." He patted the monitor board as though it were a large dog and nodded to the technicians. "Cut off the feed pump, trigger the sealer, and pull out container one." He turned back to the crew. "Now—if two of you gentlemen can carry container one down to the galley—"

Fishman Nielsen and a radar mechanic stepped forward to take the heavy plastic cylinder from the two technicians. It was about four feet long, two feet in diameter, and painted bright orange. Stenciled in white letters on it was *Processed Food Product—Experimental Use Only.*

Cheever couldn't help thinking that they might have found something more encouraging to write on the container. However, as long as it tasted all right—

The spectators drifted away, and McNeil and the technicians sat down to watch the processor start on its next batch. Cheever sat on one of the folding chairs along the bulkhead to watch them for a few minutes longer.

He was also listening for something. O'Hara would be opening the container as soon as it was delivered to the galley. If anything was wrong, they'd be able to hear him all over the ship.

Cheever looked at his watch. It had been about ten

minutes now. Plenty of time for the container to reach the galley. It had an easy-opening top, so—

"Holy mother of God, what a stink!" boomed through the ship like the crash of a depth charge. "Lord loving Jesus, get that shit out of my galley!" came next. After that there was a spectacular burst of curses and callings on all the saints.

Cheever looked at McNeil. The scientist's face was expressionless, but the captain could see the other's jaw muscles working again. For a moment it looked as though McNeil was going to kick the processor again. Not to get it started this time—more like the hero of a kung-fu movie polishing off the last villain.

Then he turned, his shoulders sagging, and looked at Cheever.

"Back to the drawing board, goddammit!" he said wearily.

"Take her up to periscope depth," said Lukin. "And raise the radar mast."

"Yes, Comrade Captain," said the officer of the watch. The planesman moved his wheel, and the depth gauge responded accordingly. *Thunderbolt* was coming up out of the depths, for a final radar bearing on the Iceland coast. Lukin was confident it would show that they were in position to turn south, toward the Atlantic.

He stepped to the periscope and squatted to meet the eyepiece as it rose out of the well. He snapped the bronze handles down and raised the periscope to a comfortable height. For Lukin that was a good six centimeters lower than for any other officer aboard *Thunderbolt*. Then he pressed his eye to the rubber-padded eyepiece.

For a moment there was only darkness, green-tinged and swirling. Then white foam tumbled around the periscope head as it thrust up into the air. Lukin saw gray-blue waves and off on the horizon a large trawler-type vessel. A small gun was visible on her fo'c'sle.

Lukin turned aside from the periscope for a moment. His eyes skewered the officer of the watch. "There is an Icelandic patrol vessel up there, Comrade Lieutenant. Why wasn't I informed? Or has the sonar stopped working?"

"We detected the vessel some time ago, Comrade Captain. But—"

"You have been guilty of carelessness, Comrade Lieutenant. That is inexcusable. You might have endangered a ship of the Socialist motherland and ninety men more valuable than yourself. This will be mentioned after our return to port, and in the appropriate places." He saw the lieutenant turn pale. "The appropriate places" was Lukin's polite phrase for the secret police.

Before Lukin could say anything more, the radar operator broke in. "Comrade Captain, our bearing. Cape Bjangtangar, thirty-one kilometers, bearing 240 relative."

"Very good. Come about to course 180 and resume two hundred meters depth."

Lukin stepped back from the periscope as it whined down into its well, followed by the radar mast. As he walked away toward the forward end of the control room, he could already feel the deck angling down under his feet. *Thunderbolt* was seeking the deep waters again for her run out into the open Atlantic.


A knock sounded on Cheever's door.

"Come in." The door opened and Frank Bronson stepped in. "Sit down, Frank. What's the latest word on the processor and its—let's call them first fruits?"

"I hope to God they're not the best the thing can do," said Bronson. "Otherwise we may be the first submarine in the history of the U.S. Navy to have a mutiny on the high seas. Or maybe at least a food riot. The men are fairly pissed off about the business."

"What about O'Hara?"

Bronson laughed. "You should have heard him, sir."

"I did. So did everyone else on board. I suspect every fish within ten miles heard it too."

"No, sir, I mean what he said afterward. He was going on, running through the saints again. Then he said he ought to call on the little people to come and take that damned processor to pieces and shove it out the garbage disposal. He'd have no more of that—shit—it put out in his galley, not without a direct order."

"He'll get that direct order," said Cheever. Then he grinned wearily. "He'll also be told that calling up leprechauns is conduct to the prejudice of good order and discipline. That seems to cover it."

Bronson nodded. "Yeah. Like a see-through dress." Then he took a deep breath. "What about McNeil?"

"The last I saw of Doctor McNeil was his feet and about six inches of both legs. The rest of him was out of sight inside the processor."

"What did he say was wrong?"

"He didn't, and I didn't want to interrupt him to ask. But one of the technicians said McNeil was starting with the feed valve and working back."

"Starting with the feed valve?"

"Yes. Apparently they've got only a vague idea of what's wrong."

"Damn," said Bronson, without any particular heat. "What next, sir?"

"Well, if the thing can't be repaired at sea, Operation Endless Voyage is going to be ended fairly soon. But McNeil's got a whole roomful of spare parts to work with. If it can be fixed, he'll do it."

"What about us?"

"Devilfish? Well, my orders give me complete discretion as to the route to follow. I think we'll head over

83

toward Estancia Seamount in the Mid-Atlantic Ridge and cruise in circles around it for a few days. After that, we'll see. If McNeil's got the processor fixed so we can go on, we'll head south."

# 12

"Is that your ride, Connie?" asked Sergeant Gonzales. He pointed to a pair of headlights creeping up the driveway toward the gate of Complex One.

Connie shaded her eyes against the glare and tried to make out the car behind the lights. "Yes, that dark-brown Chevy. That's Peter. Thank you, Sergeant. You can go now."

Gonzales smiled. "Excuse me, but my orders were more exact. I was not to let you out of my sight until you were in Peter's car. I obey orders."

Connie looked so indignant that Gonzales half expected her to stamp her foot on the concrete of the driveway. He hoped she would not. He did not want to hand her over to her fiancé in a blazing temper.

But she only said, "Honestly, Sergeant Gonzales, I can take care of myself. I don't need to be chaperoned like this."

"It is not to chaperone you, Connie. It is to avoid any danger of what almost happened to Doctor McNeil happening to you."

"There isn't any danger of that," said the girl. "You

military people are always seeing shadows and making everybody else scared of them."

"When there is a shadow, there is usually something making it, Connie. And it is the things that make the shadows that we worry about. You may be right. There may be no danger at all. But there may also be very great danger. We do not know. And until we know, my orders are strict."

Connie sighed. "All right, obey your orders if it makes you feel happier. Oh—here's Peter," she said, as a battered and dusty brown 1970 Chevrolet drew up in front of the two people. She ran around to the passenger's side and climbed in. Without a word or even a nod to Gonzales, Peter gunned the motor and roared off.

The sergeant sighed and looked after the taillights diminishing down the hill. It was good that Connie was getting married. A beautiful woman needed a husband. But was it good that she was marrying such a one as Peter Langer? He did not seem to have very much money, or even a reasonably good job. And he had never been in the armed forces. Certainly he was not such a husband as Gonzales would wish for his own Teresa, when she came of age to be married in two more years.

He sighed again at the ways of women and stepped back into the sentry box.

Peter drove in silence until they were several miles from Complex One. Then he turned to look at Connie, who was sitting stiff-backed in her seat with a sour expression on her face.

"Something wrong, honey?"

She sighed. "Oh, I guess not, really. It's just that they're all so—so paranoid back there. They think we're all in danger. They even wanted me to start carrying a gun."

85

"My God, what sort of Fascist bastards are they?"

Connie hesitated. In spite of her dislike for the security people and the security regulations, she wasn't quite comfortable discussing them, even with Peter. "Most of them are ex-Marines, I think. Certainly Gonzales is."

"That explains a lot. Marines are trained to be a bunch of mindless killers from the word go. Nobody ever expects them to think. What sort of danger are they talking about?"

Connie hesitated, and finally said, "Peter, isn't there anything else you want to talk about? I've left the job behind me for the evening. Can't it stay that way?"

Peter looked at her. "*Something's* bothering you, Connie. You've never clammed up like this before about the job. Have those monkeys been threatening you—security blacklist, or something like that? If they have, I'll go talk to Charlie Pender. He's assistant to—"

"I know. He's with Senator Bergen."

"You don't sound very enthusiastic about Bergen all of a sudden. You used to think—"

"Oh, Peter, never mind what I used to think. And let's not start off our evening with a quarrel. I want to go off somewhere with you where we can be all alone for once. I don't want to talk about politics or Bergen or anything like that."

Peter turned to look at the girl so quickly that he drove the car onto the shoulder and nearly into the ditch.

"Peter, for God's sake—keep your eyes on the road!"

"All right." He sounded sulky, and Connie sighed and resigned herself to a bad beginning for the evening. "But I can't see why you're so uptight all of a sudden. You talk as though they've gotten to you with their spy stories and all the rest of that shit."

There wasn't any answer the girl felt like giving to that. She reached into her handbag, pulled out a mirror and comb, and began doing running repairs on her hairdo. They drove on in silence for nearly fifteen minutes.

By that time Peter was more or less over his sulk. He also realized that they were wandering steadily north into the byroads and back lands of Maryland's eastern shore. He decided it was time to ask Connie where she wanted to go and what she wanted to do. He had some ideas of his own on that subject and hoped she agreed with them.

As he turned to look at her, he noticed the lights of a large car in the rearview mirror, holding steady about a hundred feet behind them. The other driver obviously had his brights on. Peter couldn't see a thing through the glare. Some local kid trying to be a smart-ass, he thought. He swung the Chevrolet onto a side road and gunned it. Gravel spurted, and Connie looked dubiously at him.

"What's the matter, Peter? Don't take—"

"Don't worry. Just some kid on our tail. I'm going to try to shake him."

But the other car made the turn, faster and tighter than the Chevrolet. Now it had closed the distance to something like fifty feet. Peter frowned.

"That guy's *really* playing games." He gunned the Chevrolet some more until it was bucking and rocking dangerously on the rough road.

"Peter, slow down!"

Peter's face was sweating, and his hands were so slick now that he was finding it hard to hold on to the wheel. "I don't know what that guy has on his mind."

"Could it be a gang?"

"I hope to hell not. If it is, we're in real trouble."

At this point the car behind swung out to pass, and Peter breathed a sigh of relief. Apparently the driver was through with his games. And as the car pulled up alongside the Chevrolet, Peter could see it was a

87

brand-new and very plush Buick. Not the kind of car a teen-age gang would be driving unless they had stolen it. He twisted his neck, trying to get a good look at the people in the other car without losing control of his own.

Before he could make them out, the other car suddenly swerved to the right. It nudged the Chevrolet hard, hard enough so that Peter heard metal buckle. The left headlight of the Chevrolet dimmed and went out, and the car swung wildly off onto the shoulder of the road.

"Shit!" Peter exploded.

Connie's face had turned the color of milk, and she was biting down hard on her lower lip. "Peter, I think—" she began. Then the Buick swung sideways again as Peter tried to steer the Chevrolet back onto the road. Again the two cars slammed into each other side-on, with a tremendous grind and tearing of metal. Peter nearly lost control of his car. Connie screamed.

"Peter, I think they may be after me."

"Who's 'they'?"

"The Russians."

"The Russians? Are you crazy?"

"No, I—" Another horrible crunch of metal. Peter was almost used to it now. He noticed that the Buick was also beginning to show signs of wear and tear. He was almost tempted to try bumping those characters off the road.

The two cars ran along side by side for a minute, while Connie spoke quickly. "The Russians are interested in where I'm working. It's a secret. They're after me, not you. If you stop and let me out, they'll take me and—"

"No way, Connie. They'll kill you! I'm going to get us out of this and—"

The Buick swung right again, and this time the shock caught Peter by surprise. He lost control. The

Chevrolet swung wildly off onto the shoulder, then kept on going. It hurtled nose-first into the ditch, slammed into the far bank, and flipped upward on its nose. Connie screamed.

Peter barely heard her. As the car crashed into the bank his seat belt broke and he was hurled against the unrecessed steering column. He felt his jaw smash, his ribs crack, pain tear through his guts as internal organs were mashed and squeezed out of shape.

Connie's seat belt held. She was hurled forward and smacked her face into the unpadded dashboard, but she suffered nothing worse than a broken nose. With blood dripping down her face, she turned to look at Peter. She screamed a second time as she saw the bleeding doll that was crumpled over the steering wheel. Frantically she clawed at the snaplock of her seat belt, trying to get free, to help Peter. Fear for him completely wiped out fear for herself.

Then her door was wrenched open and four strong arms grabbed her. She tried to scream one more time, but one of those arms suddenly sprouted a fist that smashed into her mouth. She tasted the blood from cut lips and broken teeth added to the blood from her broken nose. She choked and gagged and whimpered.

The arms were pulling her out of the car now, and she twisted and writhed. Above her she could see two faces—faces with only eyes and mouths showing through black ski caps. A hand reached across in front of her to grab the shoulder of her jacket. She bit at it. Someone howled, then a fist sank like a rod of iron into her stomach. She doubled up with a gasp and writhed helplessly in the grip of the men. The hand came in again, pulling at her jacket, then grasping the shoulder of her blouse. A quick rip, and it was torn down to her waist. Her right arm was bare and tightly held in hands that gripped her like steel claws. She

89

opened her mouth to scream again as a needle drove into her arm with savage force.

She did scream then, for the needle seemed to be shooting molten metal into her veins. Then the burning faded, and she realized that everything else was fading also. She whimpered deep in her throat as she felt the needle jerked out. She bit her mangled lips, trying to hold on to consciousness as lethargy flowed through her. Then she had to give up and let herself slide inevitably down into blackness.


Peter was holding on to consciousness by a thread as he watched four ski-capped men carry Connie's limp and bloody form past. It would be so easy to drift off and get away from the pain that was filling him. His body was just one great mass of pain. He had the horrible feeling that if he didn't become unconscious soon the pain was going to burst his body like an overripe fruit. Then he would dissolve all over the seat of the Chevrolet and die.

Two of the men were coming over toward him now. He closed his eyes and tried to go as limp as possible. Maybe Connie was right. Maybe these were Russian spies. Even if they weren't, he felt certain that they would kill him if they thought he wasn't dead already.

The approaching footsteps stopped just outside his window. A voice said, "Finish him off?"

"No," another voice said. "If he isn't dead now, he'll certainly be gone before anyone comes. We can let him die. There's no chance that way of anyone suspecting anything but natural death. There won't be anything but natural death." The man laughed, and Peter heard his footsteps receding.

There won't be any death at all, you son of a bitch, said Peter to himself. I'm going to stay alive long enough to do something to catch you. Something, somehow, no matter what.

90

© Lorillard 1975

# Come for the filter...

A PRODUCT OF
*Lorillard*

KENT
WITH
THE FAMOUS MICRONITE FILTER

DELUXE LENGTH

18 mg. "tar," 1.2 mg.
nicotine av. per cigarette,
FTC Report Oct. '74.

© Lorillard 1975

# ...you'll stay for the taste.

DELUXE LENGTH

K E N T

WITH THE FAMOUS MICRONITE FILTER

A lot of good taste
that comes easy
through the
Micronite filter.

18 mg. "tar," 1.2 mg.
nicotine av. per cigarette,
FTC Report Oct. '74.

He heard the doors of the other car slam and its engine start up. He raised his head to see its taillights receding down the road and then winking out. But before it vanished, he saw the license plate. It was a Maryland plate.

"GB7294," he said to himself. "GB7294. GB7294." He was determined to go on repeating it until he had it fixed in his mind beyond any danger of forgetting.

"GB7294. GB7294."

## 13

Admiral Cappel was suffering from insomnia. It wasn't something that happened to him very often. Usually he could go to sleep as promptly and relax as completely as any old tomcat.

But tonight was muggy, even for summer in Washington. The air conditioner was fighting a rear-guard action against the heat—and losing. *Devilfish* was much on Cappel's mind, and so was Senator Bergen and what he might do to the submarine and O.S.S.O. And to Johnny Cheever. If Bergen really went on the warpath, he could blackmark for promotion everybody connected even slightly with the project. That didn't matter to Cappel—he was long past worrying about promotion and pay. But people like Cheever and Bronson were another matter. Bronson ought to make at least captain before he went out, and Cheever—

For a moment Cappel conjured up a picture of an older, more lined, grayer John Cheever wearing the four stars of a full admiral. Then he laughed. Johnny wouldn't become President of the United States if it took him away from the submarines he loved. But he certainly had a long way to rise yet, and it would be a crime against both Cheever and the United States if Bergen screwed up his career!

So Cappel's thoughts ran on as he leafed through the latest *Jane's Fighting Ships* and back issues of the *U.S. Naval Institute Proceedings*. They refreshed him, as they always did. As long as warships sailed the seas and naval officers argued theories of leadership and civil-military relations, the world couldn't be going completely to the dogs.

Then the bedside telephone rang.

Cappel swore—he had just begun to feel sleepy—and picked up the phone. A moment later he wasn't sleepy at all.

"Yes—by all means—of course they'll think this is an emergency, but isn't it, damn it? Helicopters and everything else. Right. I'll be on my way as soon as I get some clothes on."

He sprang out of bed and ran to the closet for his clothes. As he pulled them on, he cursed every button and zipper that delayed him by so much as a split-second. Damn the Russians! Another snatch, and this time on Connie. McNeil at least was a grown man, but Connie was—

Probably dead or dying by now, a small, grim voice in his head put in.


There was nothing desperately urgent, so John Cheever was sitting in *Devilfish's* wardroom, drinking coffee and trying not to think about fresh doughnuts.

The intercom buzzer sounded. Cheever reached over and flicked it on.

"This is the radio room. Is the captain there?"

"This is the captain speaking. What's up, Pucinski?"

Cheever had trained himself to recognize most of the men of *Devilfish*'s crew by their voices. He reasoned the same way as the people who had the watch-standers in the control room learn to work blindfolded. There were times when you might badly need to work in the dark.

Radioman 1/c Pucinski seemed to be hesitating. "It's a priority one signal from Evergreen State. Captain's eyes only."

"I'm on my way." Cheever shoved his coffee cup one way and his chair the other, then stood up and headed aft toward the radio room. He briefly considered the various things that could lie behind such a message from Evergreen State. That was the code name for Admiral Cappel. Most of these things threatened an early end to the Endless Voyage.

That would be a damned shame, all things considered. Particularly when McNeil had said the processor was just about ready to go back on the line. Granted, McNeil was an optimist about his mechanical child. But Cheever was certain that McNeil would never exaggerate or lie on the subject. If McNeil said the processor was about ready to start up again, it was.

Cheever reached the radio room and took the message envelope from Pucinski. He fought back his eagerness to tear it open and satisfy his curiosity—and concern—until he was back in the privacy of his cabin.

Evergreen State To Principal. Priority one top secret. Captain's eyes only. Opposition snatch of Constance Gilman 0940. Search in progress by all appropriate agencies. Take necessary precautions at your discretion.

"Damn!" Cheever said. For him that was as much of a release of emotion as ten minutes of cursing would

93

have been for most men. Of all the dirty, filthy things to do—!

But there was nothing he could do to help Connie. The thing to consider was the "necessary precautions" that Cappel had let him choose.

First of all, tell the crew that Endless Voyage and Devilfish were even higher priority targets for the Russians than had previously been suspected. Start with Frank Bronson and work on down. Never mind the "captain's eyes only"—he could and would stretch a point of regulations in the interest of keeping his crew informed. They deserved to know if the cold war in the deep seas was suddenly about to get much hotter.

He wouldn't need to warn the sound men and the rest of the watchers to keep extra alert once they knew what was up. They would take care of that on their own. Too bad Devilfish didn't have her war crew aboard, an extra fifteen officers and men. That would distribute some of the extra work more evenly.

Fortunately, they didn't need to hot-bunk aboard Devilfish. Every man had his own sleeping space. But he'd have to see that the men coming off or going on watch got first crack at the hot food and coffee.

And he'd have to run a full-scale test of all Devilfish's operational capabilities. Speed, diving, maneuvering, silent running, sonar and hydrophone target tracking—the works. Double-check every man and routine and system for any weaknesses that might have developed since the end of the last cruise.

He must also warn Doctor McNeil that the Endless Voyage might suddenly be sailing through some very troubled waters. Cheever couldn't help wondering how McNeil would react, and the technicians as well. They had come aboard for what they thought would be a routine peacetime cruise. There had been no reason for them to think otherwise, back then. But there'd been some changes made all of a sudden. Would McNeil's apparently good adjustment suddenly fall apart and stick *Devilfish* with a first-class psychological trauma case? Cheever didn't think so. But he wished he could be more sure.

Check all the weaponry, above all—torpedoes, launchers, diving gear, and the rest. Just in case. And Cheever was convinced it was impossible to train too thoroughly on *Devilfish*'s weaponry.

*Devilfish* did not launch her torpedoes from conventional tubes, the way previous nuclear submarines had. She dove too deep to permit that. So designing her torpedo-launching gear had been a knotty problem. In fact, Cappel had said that *Devishfish*'s designers had very nearly given up on the whole problem and sent her to sea as an unarmed experimental submarine. But Cappel had thundered and roared and sent them back to their drawing boards.

It was somebody's remembering an elementary technical fact that had solved the problem. *Devilfish*'s torpedoes were designed to stand as much pressure as the ship herself, right? Right. So why not carry them outside? Submarines had done it before and during World War II. Why not do it again?

Why not indeed? The designers had stayed at their boards and come up with a remarkably ingenious solution.

In each of *Devilfish*'s two great wings was a long, double-tiered rack. In the lower tier were cradles for twenty-five assorted torpedoes. In the upper tier was a mechanical grab arrangement on cables.

When *Devilfish* went into action, the torpedo officer would select the type and number of torpedoes he wanted to fire and punch the figures into the fire control computer. The signal would shoot out to the mechanical grabs, and they would run up and down, hoisting torpedoes out of their cradles. The cables would then haul the "fish" up to the two firing cylinders.

A spring-loaded rammer would shove the two torpedoes into the two cylinders. Then a small explosive charge would go off at the rear of the tube. The water inside the tube would turn to steam and blast the torpedo out into the water. Once out, the torpedo's rockets, engines, wire-guides, or whatever would take over. It would race off through the ocean on its deadly errand.

*Devilfish* could not fire an entire salvo of six or eight "fish" at once, admittedly. But when torpedoes unerringly home in by sound or are guided all the way by impulses sent through wires and perhaps carry nuclear warheads to boot—how many are needed? *Devilfish* could carry more than twice as many torpedoes as any other nuclear submarine, and there was room to install another set of racks, to raise her capacity to over a hundred. An atomic submarine's real cruising range in wartime is until she runs out of torpedoes. *Devilfish* could go a long way.

But suppose a torpedo was defective? someone had asked. But that someone had been answered too. Each torpedo cradle was fitted with solid-state electronic monitors that could detect any malfunction in the torpedo. If a torpedo had to be down-lined for repairs, the grabs and cable hauled it up beyond the firing cylinders to storage bays. Then at a convenient time *Devilfish* would surface and the torpedo would be hauled out of the bay and down the main service hatch into the torpedo workshop. There it could not only be repaired, but practically rebuilt from scratch.

Testing weaponry was the last item on Cheever's mental checklist for putting *Devilfish* on a war footing. He shoved the message into his desk drawer, then locked the drawer and buzzed for the executive officer.

Commander Lukin was asleep; the messenger woke him.

"Comrade Captain?"

"Yes?"

"A message from Granite."

"Granite" was the code name for Admiral Barsukov. It seemed appropriate. Lukin sat bolt upright in his bunk, something a man only an inch or two taller could never have done. He snatched the message from the sailor and shot a glare at the man. The sailor vanished. Lukin leaned back and contemplated the message.

It was most interesting. The submarine W-211 had intercepted an operational signal to an American nuclear submarine operating submerged in her vicinity. Decoded by Barsukov's cryptographers, the message appeared to refer to a KGB illegal operation against some shore facility connected with this submarine.

The only such facility that was scheduled to be the target for such an operation was the Office of Special Submarine Operations, which was involved with the mysterious super-submarine *Devilfish*. So Barsukov suggested that the submarine receiving the signal was probably *Devilfish*.

Lukin growled an oath. He could have concluded that himself. Barsukov had no need to treat him like a child who had to be led by the hand to wisdom.

Had the captain of W-211 made any effort to track the American submarine? Lukin wondered, and read on. By some miracle, the captain of W-211 had kept his wits about him. He had tracked the submarine as long as he could keep within sonar range of her. She was running fast and deep, on course 150 true.

Lukin looked at the position of the contact again and then at his chart of the Atlantic. He drew a line along course 150 true from the reported positions—and his thin lips curled in a smile. *Devilfish*—if it was her—was on course to pass within fifty kilometers of Estancia Seamount. She was heading for the South Atlantic.

Very good. So would *Thunderbolt*. Lukin climbed out of his bunk and began to dress, while he started mentally calculating the necessary changes in course and speed to intercept *Devilfish*. To intercept *Devilfish*, and win him the Gold Star of a Hero of the Soviet Union.

It was a navy helicopter from the Naval Air Station at Patuxent that found the abandoned Buick. Admiral Cappel listened over the radio as they drifted in to land in the nearest field and sent an armed party to the car.

"—squad with Crowley in command is at the car now. They've got it surrounded, but—no, there doesn't seem to be anybody there. It looks—no, wait a minute. They've seen something inside. Crowley is reaching inside and pulling it out. It's—oh, Jesus, it's the girl. She's dead and naked and all covered with—"

Cappel slammed his hand down on the radio switch, cutting off the dreadful description. His other hand closed around an issue coffee cup on the corner of his desk. The hand tightened until the heavy porcelain suddenly collapsed with a pop. Pieces tinkled to the floor.

Cappel surged to his feet. He couldn't have stayed in his seat a moment longer to become Chief of Naval Operations. He headed for the door, throwing a quick glance back at his secretary.

"I'm going over to Bethesda. I want to see how Peter Langer's doing."

The secretary nodded. She understood what was going on in Cappel's mind. Peter Langer was by some miracle still alive. It was even possible that he was going to stay that way. If he did, chances of capturing those—there really wasn't any word bad enough for them—who had killed Connie Gilman were a good deal better than they might have been otherwise.

## 14

The depth gauge on the control board was hovering around 11,600 feet. *Devilfish* could go down another mile, but around here the bottom didn't. At 11,600 feet she was no more than three hundred feet above the bottom. Cheever watched the holographic display for indications of what kind of bottom they were approaching. Around here it was ooze, nine chances out of ten. But that tenth chance might be a rock.

"Dead slow," said Cheever. The speed indicator dropped back until it was just barely moving. So was *Devilfish*. With only a few tons of positive buoyancy, she almost hung between the miles of water above and the ooze below. There might be miles of that ooze too, Cheever realized. It had lain there for millions of years, slowly accumulating, undisturbed except perhaps by undersea volcanoes and occasional sinking ships settling into it. There was always a certain degree of risk in a deep bottoming because of the ooze. But it would be a standard maneuver for *Devilfish* in wartime, or at least they hoped it would be. The only way to find out for sure was to try it now.

"Switch on the lights," said Cheever.

The chief of the watch twisted a large knob with a fan-shaped, raised pattern on its plastic face. Above the holograph cube four yard-wide TV screens suddenly lit up. A moment later all four showed identical pictures of slowly swirling grayness. White flecks in the grayness were bits of organic matter drifting down from above and other bits churned up from the bottom by *Devilfish*'s churning propellers.

Then it appeared on all four screens simultaneously —a flat plain of featureless gray, with only the faintest and most shadowy humps and undulations.

"Bottom in sight," said the officer of the watch.

"Steady as she goes," replied Cheever. He pressed the button for the PA system.

"All hands, prepare to bottom." Then he took a firm grip on the back of the chair of the officer of the watch. "Flood number 4 tank."

*Devilfish* quivered faintly as more tons of water rushed into her ballast tanks. In seconds her last positive buoyancy was gone. As slowly as a snowflake, with only the faintest vibration to indicate she was under power at all, she glided down through the last two hundred feet of water and settled into the ooze. Swirling grayness momentarily blotted out the TV screens. Cheever looked at the depth gauge.

"0914," he recorded for the log. "On bottom at 11,-799 feet. Position as at 0910. All crew and systems functioning normally." He shut off the log recorder and turned to Bronson, who was standing behind him, looking over his shoulder at the TV screens.

"We'll stay down here until"—he looked at his watch—"call it 1300, then do a torpedo-firing drill and return to cruising depth and speed." He punched the intercom button again. "Sound room, this is the captain. Do we still have that deep scattering layer over us?"

"Holding firm and holding depth, sir. No problems there."

"Good." Nearly two miles above *Devilfish* a deep scattering layer—DSL—of plankton, squid, and other small marine life forms hung in the sea. It effectively scattered and blocked any sonar pulses coming down from above it. It was long odds against there being any submarines cruising in this area deep enough to be under the DSL. So there would likely be no curious or hostile sonars around to pick up the unusual phenomenon of a large submarine operating at high speed two miles down. By the time *Devilfish* broke through the DSL, she would be at a depth and speed at which she could not be distinguished from a conventional nuclear submarine.

"Frank, you take her while we're on the bottom," said Cheever. "I want to talk to McNeil."

"Aye aye, sir," said the executive officer. Cheever headed aft toward the processor's compartment, walking slowly, one step at a time, to set the example for the crew. His feet in their padded-sole sandals made practically no noise.

As he walked aft Cheever decided he would have Bronson run the torpedo-firing exercise too. Frank was a damned fine officer, with an ebullience, a joy in life, and a range of physical skills that Cheever couldn't help envying. But he needed to be shaken just a little out of his willingness to follow Cheever's lead. Frank was unlikely ever to go higher than captain, no matter what. But with a little pushing he would be the ideal man to take command of the next *Devilfish*-type submarine.

If there was a next one. That was still very much up in the air, and it would be for quite a while longer. Cheever wondered how Admiral Cappel was getting along with—or against—Senator Bergen.

McNeil met Cheever at the door of the experimental module compartment, grinning from ear to ear. "Captain, we're ready to start up any time now." His voice was loud and triumphant.

Cheever held a finger to his lips. "We're under silent-operating conditions, Doctor. Don't shout, please."

The smile vanished from McNeil's face. For a moment Cheever thought he might be going to snap back. But apparently the scientist's self-control was holding better than that. Instead, he asked, "Does that mean we can't start up the processor?"

Cheever couldn't help feeling that McNeil sounded a little like a small boy asking why he couldn't have more candy. He didn't altogether blame McNeil—the troubles with the processor must have been maddening to the scientist. For McNeil the whole purpose of the voyage, and for the time being, of Devilfish herself, revolved around the processor.

Reluctantly, Cheever nodded. "It will have to stay shut down until we're back to cruising speed and depth. We can't have any unnecessary noise."

McNeil shrugged and turned away. Cheever thought he heard the scientist mutter something about "damned war games" as he turned. But he couldn't be sure enough to make an issue of it. Still, he wished he could be more sure that McNeil wasn't going to be a problem again. It wasn't a matter of the scientist's general stability now—that didn't worry Cheever. It was McNeil's fanatical dedication to the success of the processor.

The young naval surgeon handling Peter Langer's case was waiting in his office at Bethesda Naval Hospital when Admiral Cappel arrived.

"Good morning, sir."

"What's good about it? No, cancel that." Cappel knew that he must look as though he had been suffering from insomnia for weeks instead of days. He also knew that he almost felt as if he had. He sat down and looked at the surgeon. "What's the prospect?"

The surgeon rubbed eyes that were nearly as red as the admiral's and hesitated. He had been up all night too, working even harder than Cappel, patching up Peter Langer's battered body. He was a youngish lieutenant-commander, no more accustomed to coping with admirals, even retired ones, on no sleep than lieutenant-commanders usually are. He was obviously picking his words with care as he spoke.

"Broken left arm, broken collarbone, broken jaw and cheekbone with several teeth missing. Probable concussion. Compound fractures of five ribs. Possible internal injuries—"

"Why possible?"

"With an impact on the torso like this, they're always possible. But we haven't detected any internal bleeding or any loss of kidney or liver function yet. And if they haven't showed up yet, it's a halfway decent chance they won't."

"I see."

"He's also suffering from severe shock, naturally. He's a very lucky man. If that car had been traveling any faster or hit anything more solid, the fractured ribs would have pierced his heart or lungs. He would have been DOA."

"How soon will he be able to talk?"

"Talk?" The surgeon couldn't quite manage to retain his awe of admirals when they started asking stupid questions about medical matters. "Admiral Cappel, it's only been in the last two hours that I've been reasonably sure of being able to keep him alive. He looked god-awful when the copter brought him in, and he still looks pretty lousy. He's not even out of the woods yet, let alone able to answer questions." Then he appeared to remember to whom he was saying this. "I'm sorry, sir, but—"

Cappel cut him off with a raised hand. "Never mind, Doctor. It's been a long night for both of us, and longer for you than for me. So—what have you done?"

The doctor ran down the list. Transfusions, immobilization of the fractures. Pain-killers, broad-spectrum antibiotics, stimulants. Peter Langer had received very thorough treatment.

"Good. Doctor, I trust you realize there are national security aspects to this affair?"

The surgeon nodded. "I suspected that when I heard that a civilian who'd been in an auto accident was being flown here to Bethesda. Is there—is there anything special I need to know?"

Cappel shook his head. "Nothing. I'll rely on you to take the basic precautions normal in cases like this. Security-cleared nurses and the rest. However, I'm also going to ask you to put up with a round-the-clock armed guard on the man."

The doctor's eyebrows rose. "Is he that dangerous, in his present condition? What about the risk to the—"

"It isn't Peter Langer who's dangerous, except possibly to some people who are responsible for his being here now. But they may be dangerous to him. So I'm sending over some men from the security detail of my office to reinforce the watch."

The doctor's face was expressionless. He was obviously thinking over the possible implications of a security matter so critical that the regular hospital staff couldn't be trusted. Just as obviously, he didn't like them. The hunched shoulders and the hands that twisted a pencil round and round made that unmistakable.

But like John Cheever, the doctor was in and of the United States Navy. He knew the navy's response to all orders, no matter how odd they might seem.

"Aye aye, sir," he said, and stood up to see Admiral Cappel out of the office.

## 15

Cheever stood in the control room of *Devilfish* and watched the depth gauge. The submarine was rising past the two-thousand-foot level now. By Cheever's orders, she was rising as slowly as a balloon, both engines stopped, silent conditions set. After the initial blowing of tanks to start *Devilfish* rising from the bottom, Cheever had blown no more ballast. Trim was maintained by sending men running fore and aft, as bow or stern began to rise too fast.

As silently as a bubble, *Devilfish* rose out of the depths. She would give off no sound to betray her presence to any curious or hostile ears within listening range. If somebody was pinging with sonar, of course, she would show up on their screens eventually. But a sonar impulse from the surface could not get through the deep scattering layer that still lay some five hundred feet above them. By the time *Devilfish* rose through the DSL and started her engines, there would once again be nothing to distinguish her from any other late-model nuclear submarine.

Cheever cracked his knuckles to release some of his tension. The full runthrough of *Devilfish*'s capabilities had been a twelve-hour grind for every man on board. It would be good when they were back at cruising depth and speed. It would be even better now that they knew *Devilfish* was fully combat-ready. Her systems were all working at top efficiency, and that included her crew.

Now that they were heading back to cruising depth, the processor could also start up again. That would make Doctor McNeil as happy as a child turned loose in a candy store.

Cheever decided to go aft and see how the scientist and his team were doing under the strain of battle-readiness conditions. *Devilfish* was only rising about fifty feet a minute. It would be another half hour before she reached normal cruising depth.

Cheever was turning away from the control center when the intercom light went on.

"Control room, captain speaking."

"Sound room, sir." Cheever recognized the voice of Chief Sonarman Kitter. "We're getting underwater propeller noises bearing approximately 320, fifty rpm. It sounds like another sub, running slow and deep, sir."

"No sign of pinging?"

"None so far, sir."

Cheever frowned. Kitter was one of the best soundmen he'd ever encountered, with fifteen years' experience in listening to the strange noises the sea makes. That was important now. The natural sounds of the sea and its teeming life can duplicate almost any manmade noise under the right circumstances. Mating whales, curious dolphins, masses of shrimp have all caused confusion and alarm aboard surface ships and submarines of a dozen nations.

Kitter knew this. He could sort out a manmade noise from its natural imitators nine times out of ten. If he said that the new noise sounded like a submarine, then it probably was a submarine.

If so, whose? There were not supposed to be any American submarines in this area now, not for at least another three days. So it was good odds that it was a foreign submarine, probably nuclear if she was running this deep.

That meant Devilfish would have to be even more careful than before. Even friendly foreign governments weren't yet on the list of people who were supposed to know about Devilfish's capabilities. That included both the British and the French, who had nuclear submarines and occasionally sent them through this area. Not often, but sometimes. Just often enough to confuse the picture a little.

Nonetheless, it was probable that an unidentified nuclear submarine in this area at this time was Russian. And that meant that matters could suddenly become extremely delicate and even deadly in a matter of minutes.

Any intention Cheever had had of leaving the control room vanished in a split second.

He turned to Frank Bronson.

"We've got unidentified propeller noises, probably a submarine, bearing 320. Deep and slow."

"Think it's a Russian, sir?"

"It's too soon to tell. But I think we'd better assume that it is."

"The one looking for us?"

"She could be, if there is one. But we don't know that the Russians have taken any action along those lines."

"After two snatches at Complex One? They must be doing something."

"Maybe. But if they are, it could be as snarled up in red tape as any project of ours. Still, I'm with you. We'll assume it's a Russian on the prowl for Devilfish until we get positive proof to the contrary." He cracked his knuckles again. "Pass the word along those lines, quietly but as fast as you can. I don't want any excitement, but I do want everybody extra alert. It will help if they know that our newfound friend out there may suddenly start playing rough."

Bronson nodded. "Can do, sir. Any other orders?"

Cheever considered various possibilities for a moment. "No. If he's not pinging, he may be hoping he can avoid being detected for a while. There's no point in starting our own sonar and disillusioning him. And we've got to get up at least another five hundred feet before I'm willing to make any sound louder than somebody pulling on a skivvy shirt. We'll just sit tight and quiet and let him make the first move."

"Aye aye, sir."

At a bare nine knots *Thunderbolt* slipped through the deep waters. Five hundred meters below the surface, she was near her normal operational limits. Only a hundred meters farther down the pressure of the water would collapse her massive hull like a tin can and send her and her ninety men drifting down through three kilometers of blackness to the ooze on the bottom.

Commander Lukin was aware of the statistics of *Thunderbolt's* present situation, but only as statistics. They had no emotional meaning for him whatever.

Some of the other men in the control room weren't so calm. Lukin could see sweat on faces, fingers run around inside collars, tongues licking dry lips. Definitely the most fragile part of *Thunderbolt* was likely to be her crew. They were not steel as she was—or as Lukin had made himself.

He leaned back in the commanding officer's chair and punched the intercom for the sound room.

"Still no indications?"

"None, Comrade Captain."

Lukin was beginning to suspect either inadequate listening gear or an inadequate man at it. The American submarine—best not call her *Devilfish* yet, tempting though it was—had to be somewhere in this area. And she had to be under power and therefore at least somewhat detectable. The bottom was too deep for her to drop down and sit quietly on it until *Thunderbolt* went away.

Unless—*Devilfish*—could dive nearly four kilometers and survive. That was a thought, one Commander Lukin did not find particularly pleasant.

An hour had passed. Cheever was sitting on his bunk, leaning back against the pastel blue section of hull that formed one side of the bunk alcove. Outside that hull was a thousand feet of water.

*Devilfish* had risen almost inch by inch since Kitter picked up the Russian submarine. Cheever had carefully bled air out of one of the ballast tanks until the submarine had only a few tons of positive buoyancy. Now she rose as slowly as a piece of waterlogged wood, barely five hundred feet an hour.

The air had been bled in very slowly and carefully, to reduce the danger of the Russians' picking up the noise. It had been a pleasure to watch Chief Nielsen at the ballast board, playing the switches as delicately as a brain surgeon used his instruments. The Russian showed no signs of having heard anything—but he showed no signs of leaving either.

"All right," said Cheever. "Our friend is obviously doing a search of this area. A search means he's looking for something. Can you think of anything else besides us that he might be looking for?"

Bronson shook his head. "Not without pinging, I can't."

"My feeling exactly. Let's assume that he's looking for us and work from there. Right at the moment we've got the advantage because we know he's there and so far he doesn't seem to have picked us up. But we can't go anywhere fast without his knowing about it and possibly getting ideas."

"Are you sure?" said Bronson. "Those Russian subs are a hell of a lot noisier than ours, and *Devilfish* is even quieter than the rest of our A-subs. No gear noises and all the rest. Besides that, his listening gear won't be as good as ours."

"I know. But I still doubt if we could do more than twelve, fifteen knots without being picked up. And that's too slow to get us out of this area very fast."

"We could just go back down deep again," said Bronson. "We can lie doggo on the bottom here, even if he can't."

"We could," said Cheever. "But our friend is under the DSL. Suppose he stops playing a waiting game, starts pinging, and picks up his long-awaited target—seven thousand feet down. He'll have one of the bits of data he probably wants handed to him on a silver platter. And the nearest piece of bottom within normal depth limits is on the slopes of Estancia Seamount. That's sixty miles away."

Cheever stood up and reached past Bronson for the piece of sponge cake on his desk. When a combat-type situation was setting in, the reins he tried to keep on his sweet tooth tended to loosen.

Between bites of the cake, he finished his thinking out loud. It was more talking than he usually did. In fact, it was more than he ever did, except when Frank Bronson was around. Frank Bronson did a lot of things, but one of the most important was to serve as an audience. Not an uncritical one, because he would tell Cheever if he thought his captain was talking nonsense. (Cheever didn't want an uncritical audience anyway.) Frank Bronson sitting there listening served to take the edge off Cheever's loneliness as captain, the man who finally had to say yes or no. But he still had to say it.

"We've got a Russian out there who's looking for us. There's no safe way to just evade, without either risking detection or revealing *Devilfish*'s capabilities."

He cracked his knuckles. "So we're not going to evade. We're going to start dropping hints that we're here until our friend picks them up. If he doesn't do anything after that, we'll go on about our business and he'll go on about his. But if he decides to trail us—well, we'll be sure that he's the one we're looking for."

Bronson nodded. Cheever swallowed the last of the cake, and the two officers rose and went out into the passageway. As they walked back to the control room, Cheever was turning his decision over and over in his mind, examining it from all possible angles.

It made sense. Granted, it would interfere somewhat with the Endless Voyage. There might be trouble with running the processor if they had to operate silently for a long time. And if that happened, there might also be trouble with Doctor McNeil, even apart from what the tension might do to the scientist. There was a risk of scandal, and of failure for the processor.

On the other hand, there was a much greater risk to everything if they had to cruise around in ignorance of how much the Russians knew about O.S.S.O. and its projects. Even worse, in ignorance of what the Russians might be prepared to do to *Devilfish*.

Considering how rough they had been willing to play around Complex One, it was good odds they would be willing to play even rougher out at sea. Down deep, all sorts of things could happen or be made to happen without leaving any evidence to prove anything.

As Cheever reached the control room, he was satisfied that he had made the right decision.

Lukin himself was in the sound room of *Thunderbolt*, with earphones clamped to his small head, when he heard it. He was not an expert soundman; he admitted that, at least to himself. But it didn't take an expert soundman to pick up what was coming in from the sea outside, or to identify it.

"Propeller noises," he said coolly. "Single screw, widely varying rpm. Bearing approximately 140. A submarine." He listened again. "And apparently having difficulties of some sort. She's blowing her tanks."

He took off the earphones and hung them up on the sound console. The second-in-command looked at him.

"Shall we start a sonar sweep, Comrade Captain?"

Lukin had to hesitate before he answered. "No," he finally said. "Not yet. Let's listen to what he's doing for a while. If he's having real difficulties—" He left the sentence unfinished.

The other officer finished it for him. "Perhaps we should signal him and ask if he needs assistance?"

His answer was a chill glare from Lukin. "No," the little man said again. "He is sending out no distress signal. Perhaps he is too proud to do so, knowing that there is a Russian submarine sitting by, watching his incompetence." Or perhaps he is *Devilfish*, thought Lukin. He couldn't deny that he was becoming curious on that point. Or that he would not be able to suppress that curiosity forever.


Cheever spoke into the intercom.

"Engine room. Any trouble from our switching from shaft to shaft?"

The engineer officer's reply was a chuckle. "Not a bit, sir. We can go on doing this all day."

"We won't be doing it that long," said Cheever. "Just until our friend outside either dies of unsatisfied curiosity or goes to work with his sonar."

He turned to the officer of the watch. "Flood number 2 tank. Emergency dive rate."

The lieutenant stared at him for a moment, then:

112

"Aye aye, sir." Chief Nielsen flipped the appropriate switches. *Devilfish* shuddered as tons of water poured in.

That would give the Russian soundmen one more thing to chew on. Sooner or later, the Russian should start up his sonar. If he didn't, it would strongly suggest that he wasn't here looking for anything. In that case *Devilfish* could leave the Russian behind her in a hurry without a qualm.

The deck was tilting as the water pulled *Devilfish's* bow down.

"Engine room," said Cheever. "Two-thirds ahead, port only."

"Aye aye, sir."

*Devilfish* began to swing around in a circle as her port propeller speeded up. One more antic for the Russians to hear.


Lukin was aware that everyone in *Thunderbolt's* control room was staring at him. He was also aware that even more of them had started sweating. The odor of perspiration hung strongly in air that was already heavy with increasing tension.

Who was that madman out there, and what was he doing? The sound room had already reported half an hour of the most preposterous antics Lukin had ever heard of. If it was a submarine, something must be wrong with it. But it showed no signs of rising to the surface, nor of sinking to the bottom. They hadn't heard the terrible crushing-metal noises of a submarine collapsing deep in the sea.

Lukin allowed himself a small frown. It would be revealing himself to begin a sonar sweep. But to do otherwise might be letting *Devilfish* escape. Not only unharmed, but not even adequately analyzed! That would be a failure on his part, a failure in his duty.

He made his decision.

"Sound room!"

"Yes, Comrade Captain?"

"Start a full sonar sweep."

They all heard it together—the unmistakable faint *pinnnngggg* of a sonar beam reflected from *Devilfish's* hull. It wasn't reflected as loudly as it would have been from a metal hull, but it was loud enough to be heard all over the ship—and hopefully in the earphones of the Russian soundmen.

Frank Bronson's tanned face split in a grin. Chief Nielsen laughed out loud. The planesman of the watch let out a sound like an Indian war whoop. Everybody else in the control room was smiling as though they had just been left a hundred-thousand-dollar legacy.

Cheever's smile was there, but it was thin. He had won the first skirmish with the Russian. But he had no intention of assuming the whole battle would go the same way. He hoped nobody else would either.

"All right," he said. "We know he's curious about us. Let's see how long he'll stay curious. Twenty knots, course 150, depth eight hundred."

*Devilfish* already had negative buoyancy. As the planesman of the watch twisted his controls, she began to angle deeper into the sea.

Cheever decided against securing from general quarters, for the moment at least. He wanted to find out what the Russian was up to, certainly. But he didn't want any unpleasant or fatal surprises in the meantime.

## 16

"Admiral Cappel!" said the WAVE secretary quickly. "The doctor from Bethesda's on the phone."

"Put him on." Cappel picked up the receiver. "Hello, Doctor. What's the word today? He *is*? Good! What's he saying? Anything else? All right, call me again as soon as he's in any condition to be—" Cappel rejected the word "interrogated." "As soon as I can talk to him without endangering his recovery. I don't think I need to tell you that this is top secret. Good. Thank you, Doctor." Cappel hung up and turned to the WAVE. "Get me Dave Wilton."

David Wilton was officially the senior FBI man assigned to the O.S.S.O. case. Unofficially, he was the coordinator for the whole investigation into the snatches at Complex One. Cappel knew him from the days when Wilton had handled two cases of sabotage at the New London submarine base. He had handled them skillfully, quietly, and creatively.

That was the most important thing about David Wilton. He was a creative security man. Many of the FBI's best agents weren't, to say nothing of the agents of other intelligence offices and police departments. But Wilton knew when to bend rules and when to wink at other people's bending them. That could be important in this case, considering how critical it might be to work fast.

115

Wilton was also formidably closed-mouthed, even by the standards of FBI agents, who were notoriously ungabby men. That could be even more important in this case. It was a case that could be very ticklish politically. Ticklish enough, in fact, to blow O.S.S.O. and everybody in it sky high, even if *Devilfish* brought off the Endless Voyage in textbook fashion and the processor turned out T-bone steaks.

Cappel wondered how *Devilfish* was doing. Cheever had some discretion in reporting, as long as he did so at least every forty-eight hours. It was coming up soon on forty hours since the last message from the submarine.

A couple of minutes later David Wilton was on the telephone.

"Good morning, Admiral. What can I do for you today?"

"Peter Langer has recovered consciousness. He keeps muttering "GB7294" over and over again. That's all."

"Nothing else at all?"

"Nothing."

"Too bad. However, even that helps. It sounds like a license number. I rather suspect it was the license number of the Buick involved in the operation against Ms. Gilman. The people who used it stripped off the plates and used acid on the engine serials before they abandoned it. I'll start a check right away. This may be useful."

Another of David Wilton's characteristics was to be extremely tentative and cautious in all his statements. Cappel suspected that if somebody ever blew up the White House, Wilton would start off by saying that "there appears to have been a bomb involved."

This habit didn't keep Wilton from reaching conclusions, however. And when he reached a conclusion he acted on it, quietly, competently, and with alarming efficiency. Then he became a very dangerous man. That was fine with Cappel. He very badly wanted whoever was responsible for Connie's death brought to book. For the moment, he wanted it considerably more than he wanted Senator Thomas Bergen's hide.

"I hope it will be useful," said the admiral.

"How is Mr. Langer otherwise?"

"The doctor says he's no longer in any danger, but it will be several days before it will be safe to talk to him."

"Is the doctor reliable, as far as you know?"

"As far as I know, yes. But that may not be very far. If you want to check—"

"I'll keep that in mind. But I'd rather not make any unnecessary investigations. I certainly don't want to risk coming between a doctor and a patient. We can't afford any leaks or scandals with this case, considering who may be watching all of us."

It took a moment for Cappel to realize whom Wilton meant. "Senator Bergen?"

"Who else?" Wilton chuckled. "Remember, Admiral, you aren't the only people who rub Bergen the wrong way. He doesn't much like the Bureau, either, and we—well, let's say I return the compliment."

Cappel laughed. "Four-oh, Dave. And thanks for everything."

"No trouble, Admiral." The phone clicked off.

Barsukov was reading the intelligence file on the latest French missile submarine when his secretary announced Captain Volynsky. With a grimace Barsukov shoved the file into his desk drawer and got ready to greet the fat intelligence officer as politely as possible.

"Good morning, Comrade Captain. What have you to report today?"

"The organs of state security report the illegal operation against the Office of Special Submarine Operations has been carried out. They were unable to retain the subject long enough for a complete interrogation, however."

"Did they get anything at all?" It was bad news if they hadn't. Illegal operations were risky, so unsuccessful ones were frowned on. A major failure could make the intelligence people reluctant to work with Barsukov in the future. That would be disastrous to his effectiveness.

Even if the intelligence people were still willing to cooperate, there might be pressure on them from above. There certainly would be, if there were any sort of scandal. And if there were a sufficiently large scandal, there might even be pressure directly on Barsukov.

"They were still analyzing the data when I left," said Volynsky. "At least that was what they said."

"You seem to have your doubts," said Barsukov. He disliked appearing ill at ease before this man, whom he frankly despised for everything except his intelligence skills. But the situation was potentially too dangerous for him to be entirely calm.

" think they were telling the truth," said Volynsky. "Remember, I have been around intelligence people rather more than you have. I can assess their reactions perhaps more accurately."

"Don't push me, Volynsky," growled Barsukov. "I know that you were commanding an intelligence desk when I was commanding an Arctic Fleet submarine flotilla. Don't let it go to your head, though." His left hand clacked shut, one of the pincers gouging a line along the polished top of the desk.

Volynsky shrugged. His skin was as thick as his belly. No doubt he was used to being slapped down by seagoing officers. Barsukov told himself to remember that, the next time he felt on edge. Striking at Volynsky did the fat man no harm and simply served to reveal his own short temper. If Barsukov did that too often, Volynsky might eventually have a mass of material that he could take to some receptive and powerful man. Barsukov had no illusions that he was a man much loved in high places in the Soviet Union, or without powerful enemies. And he didn't want to give them any possible weapons against him. He knew that he had too much to do yet, where he was. He also knew that when eventually he had to leave the navy for good, he would die a little. Perhaps he would simply die.

But these were morbidly bourgeois thought patterns, he told himself sharply. He turned back to Volynsky. "So we have no guarantees of any more knowledge of our mysterious friend *Devilfish* from the illegal operation?"

"That is about what I would say, Comrade Admiral."

"Very good. Then it is up to Commander Lukin and *Thunderbolt*."

Which was as it ought to be, Barsukov thought. He respected the competence of the intelligence agencies. Sometimes they did very good work. But when it came to matters concerning ships and sailors, they often seemed to be helpless. No amount of work on shore could substitute for a trained seaman and a good ship on the spot.

That reminded him—was *Thunderbolt* actually on the spot? The report based on the observations of W-211 had been sent and acknowledged. Since then *Thunderbolt* had been silent.

Was it time to ask for a progress report? Barsukov considered the idea, then decided against it. Lukin could do well enough without anyone looking over his shoulder at every moment. If something critical happened, *Thunderbolt* would be heard from at once.

Unless *Devilfish* was so advanced that she could strike down the Russian submarine in an instant, with no danger to herself or risk of detection. An ugly thought, but not a high probability. The Americans

119

lacked the ruthlessness required to conceive and execute such a move. It was a weakness that Barsukov had successfully exploited more than once.

But suppose it was a weakness that some one man high in their navy—or this mysterious O.S.S.O.—lacked. That was still not a high probability. But it was one that Barsukov could not dismiss from his mind.

## 17

When Cheever entered *Devilfish*'s control room, the first thing he saw was Frank Bronson standing behind the officer of the watch. Both men were staring at the holographic display cube. It showed a flat bottom unrolling itself nearly two miles below *Devilfish* as she ran south at a sedate twenty knots.

It also showed the Russian submarine still holding ten miles behind *Devilfish*. As far as Cheever could see, the other submarine had altered neither course, speed, distance, depth, nor bearing since he went off to his cabin to sleep five hours ago.

"I see our friend is still with us," he said. "Has he done anything worth noting lately?"

Bronson shook his head. "Don't worry, sir. I'd have told you if he had."

Cheever frowned half-humorously. "Frank, that wasn't quite what I asked. *Did* he do anything?"

Frank Bronson was like most good executive officers—he sometimes fell into the trap of trying to keep the captain's sleep unbroken regardless of what happened. Every captain had to fight this because no captain could allow it.

The captain of a ship is responsible for whatever happens to her, good, bad, or disastrous. Law, naval regulations, and traditions of the sea many centuries old all say the same on this point. So a captain has to make sure that he always knows what is going on. Otherwise, he may end up having to shoulder the blame for a ship lost or lives destroyed through a subordinate's errors.

A captain with integrity will shoulder this blame and watch his career and reputation disintegrate in stoical silence. But he doesn't enjoy it, even as he endures it. And as long as he has a ship under him, he will do everything to make sure that he can do his duty properly.

Bronson's tanned face flushed as he recognized that he had been caught off base. Most captains, in fact, would have been a good deal rougher.

"No, sir, he hasn't done a damned thing worth calling you for. He's just sitting there ten miles astern, matching our course and speed as if our controls were controlling him too. He's holding a depth about a hundred feet above ours, though." Bronson hesitated. "Do you think that means he might be one of their older A-subs, with a lighter hull?"

"It could," said Cheever. "It could also mean he's just trying to give that impression. He could be thinking that if he hangs on long enough we'll try to evade. We'll be more tempted to do that if we think he's an older A-sub that we can pull away from fairly easily. Then he can surprise us by continuing to match every move we make."

Bronson nodded. "He could also be wondering if we're an older submarine that he can run rings around if he steps up the pace. Maybe we ought to prove that we aren't. I don't like just sitting here waiting for him to play us for a sucker."

"Neither do I," said Cheever. "And we're not going to do it." He pressed the intercom.

"Engine room, this is the captain. At"—he looked at his watch—"1750, give me another forty rpm."

"Aye aye, sir."

Another forty rpm would push *Devilfish* through the water six or seven knots faster. It would be interesting to see how long it would take the Russian to notice the increase and react to it.

Cheever badly wanted to provoke that reaction. A lot depended on it. The Russian submarine might really be determined to hold position on *Devilfish*, at least long enough to test her speed capabilities; in that case, the Russian would match his speed to *Devilfish*'s as long as possible.

On the other hand, the Russian might simply be playing games out of idle curiosity or a desire to goose the Americans on general principles. The two navies had been doing that sort of thing for twenty years, ever since the Russians had had any sort of a high-seas navy. In that case, as soon as the speed pushed close to the Russian's limits, he would drop out and go on his way. So would *Devilfish*.

Cheever wasn't sure which he was hoping for. It would be much simpler to carry out Operation Endless Voyage without Russian kibitzers. On the other hand, playing games with the Russians was something he enjoyed and was more than good at. This deadly skill was one of the reasons he had been given command of *Devilfish*. And of course there was always the chance of giving a uniquely complete test to his unique ship. That was a pleasant possibility, and he suspected that every other man aboard *Devilfish* would see things exactly the same way.

However, there was one problem he could ease right

now with very little effort. He punched the intercom again.

"Module compartment, this is the captain. Is Doctor McNeil there?"

"Speaking, Captain. What's up?"

"Doctor, our Russian friend is still with us. But he's not doing anything to us, and we're not planning to do anything to him. So far as I can see, there's no reason not to start up the processor again."

McNeil's voice sounded strained, but also relieved. "Thank you, sir."

"No problem, Doctor. And good luck."

Commander Lukin was having a solitary dinner in *Thunderbolt*'s wardroom when the sound room called him.

"Comrade Captain, the American submarine has increased speed to forty kilometers an hour. He is holding course and speed, however."

"Very good."

Lukin spooned up the last of his borscht and considered this development. Was the American trying to run away from *Thunderbolt*? If so, perhaps a disagreeable surprise could be arranged for him. The American would not be particularly happy to see the sonar pulse that was *Thunderbolt* holding position on him without effort.

And if the American could run away from *Thunderbolt*? That would be a surprise for Lukin, but an agreeable one. As far as he knew, *Thunderbolt* and her sisters were the fastest nuclear attack submarines afloat. Anything much faster than *Thunderbolt* could be only one ship—*Devilfish*. It would be very satisfactory to be finally sure that the submarine ahead was his quarry. It would be even more satisfactory to start learning the limits of her performance.

Lukin pushed his chair back from the table and

snapped his orders into the intercom. "Maintain course and depth. Increase speed to forty kilometers."

An hour had passed. The two submarines were still racing south, *Devilfish* eight hundred feet down, the Russian ship seven hundred. Both were steering course 150, and both were doing nearly thirty-five knots now. That was pushing toward the limit for most ordinary nuclear submarines. But for *Devilfish* it was still an almost leisurely cruise.

Another decision was coming up for Cheever, another of those moments when the three stripes and the gold braid seemed to weigh on him like lead. He bore the weight easily, from long practice, but he never forgot it. He knew that if he ever did, he would no longer be a safe or competent submarine captain.

Increase speed again? Yes. How much? That depended still on who was following them. An older Soviet A-sub would be near her top speed now. One of the new ones that had come out in the last three or four years could certainly do forty knots, perhaps forty-five, just possibly fifty. They were fine, powerful ships of their type, even if they weren't equal to *Devilfish*.

Cheever decided to assume that the submarine behind him was one of the latest models. Unfortunately, it could be no more than an assumption. Even as good a sonar man as Kitter was could tell only so much about another submarine from its sonar pulse. Kitter was certain that it was an attack-type submarine, rather than one of the thicker and noisier missile launchers. Beyond that, it was all guesswork.

Of course *Devilfish* could still run rings around the other submarine. But the longstanding principles for operating *Devilfish* under curious or hostile eyes held. Don't give them anything from which they can draw conclusions.

On the other hand, what about matching the Russian's speed—and then a little more besides? Not much more—just a little bit, enough to give her skipper a red face and perhaps damage some of his machinery if he tried to keep up with *Devilfish*. Showing that American submarines were at least slightly faster than Russian ones certainly wouldn't be revealing any secrets about *Devilfish*. That had been an accepted fact in the U.S. submarine forces for several years.

But perhaps the Russian skipper was one of those fanatics who believed that the Russians invented the airplane and the electric light. If he was, he would tend to assume the superiority of his own ship over any American submarine.

It was time to give him a nasty surprise, in that case.

"Engine room, this is the captain. Can you increase by ten rpm at two-minute intervals until further orders, starting when I give the signal?"

"No problem, sir."

"Good. Stand by for my signal." Then he punched the intercom for the sound room.

"Have you got a good plot and speed on our friend?"

"Picture-perfect, sir," came Kitter's voice.

"Good. Keep that plot on him. We're going to do a little rat-racing with him. Let me know the *split second* he starts losing position on us." In spite of all the electronic displays *Devilfish* had, Cheever still had no reason not to trust the judgment of a good soundman as well.

In the tone of Kitter's reply Cheever could almost see the grin that must be spreading across the man's face. *Devilfish*'s crew had the same competitive instincts as their captain. Now—

"Engine room. I'm going to give you the signal." Cheever followed the second hand around the dial of his Rolex. "Thirty seconds—twenty—ten, nine, eight, seven, six, five, four, three, two, one—mark!"

The increase in speed from an extra ten rpm was barely noticeable on the speed indicator. But repeating it at two-minute intervals would rapidly add up to something impressive.

Cheever wondered what would give way first—the Russian captain's will or some vital part of his ship. Cheever didn't actually *want* to drive the Russian submarine beyond her design limits, but if it happened in the normal course of things—well—

In the control room of *Thunderbolt* Lukin watched the speed needle crawl upward and listened to the reports from the sound room. The two submarines were now racing along at nearly seventy kilometers an hour—forty-five knots. *Thunderbolt* was the fastest submarine in the Soviet navy, but she was pushing close to her limits.

The soundman came on the intercom again.

"Comrade Captain, I think the American has increased speed again." The man's voice was barely audible over the noise in the control room. The high speed was sending vibrations through *Thunderbolt's* steel frame and making the water roar past her outside. Lukin had to strain to hear.

"You *think*? You're supposed to *know*, you fool!"

"Comrade Captain, the external noise level is becoming almost more than our sonar can handle! It is becoming very hard to accurately read the signals we are getting from the American!"

Lukin was momentarily speechless at this insubordination. Then his mind churned furiously, picking words to blaze back at the soundman, threatening him with court-martial or worse.

Before he could get the words out, a petty officer burst into the control room. He dashed up to Lukin, but he had to virtually yell in the captain's ear before he could make himself heard.

"Comrade Captain," Lukin finally heard. "There's a short circuit in the ventilation motor of the forward bunkroom. We're going to have to shut it down and evacuate the compartment; otherwise, we'll have a fire in a few minutes."

"What?" exploded Lukin. "That's impossible. Who's responsible for this mess?"

"Comrade Captain," the petty officer said stubbornly, "nobody's responsible. It's this damned high-speed vibration. Must have shaken something loose somewhere. We'll have to shut down the motor before we can trace it."

The soundman came on again. "The American has definitely made another speed increase, Comrade Captain. He is doing at least seventy-four kilometers an hour now."

Lukin took several deep breaths and by heroic effort got himself temporarily under control. Then he called the engine room. "The American has made another speed increase. Match it."

"We'll try, Comrade Captain, but—"

"Yes—*but?*" There was a steel edge in Lukin's voice. The officer on watch in the engine room apparently decided against making any reply. There was only silence on the intercom. A moment later the vibration in *Thunderbolt* became even more intense and the noise even louder.

Lukin realized that the petty officer from forward had vanished. Gone back to his station, no doubt. If he shut down the motor without orders— Everybody else in the control room was staring at their captain. Lukin tried to read the expressions on the tightly controlled, sweating faces. Fear, nervousness, what? He realized he wasn't particularly good at interpreting other people's reactions. Most of his career had been spent ignoring them or overriding them. He sat down and

127

tried to tune out the noise around him. What came next? If the American made another speed increase—

Before the American could do anything or Lukin could settle his thoughts, the alarm siren split the heavy air. Lukin jumped to his feet and swung his eyes across the main control panel. The engine room board was blazing red. Then:

"Fire and flooding in the engine room!" came over the intercom. The engine-room officer sounded half hysterical.

Lukin was as cold as ice as he replied. "This is the captain. Report!"

"Flooding through the glands around the main shaft, heavy flooding. And a fire in the shaft alley itself. Heavy smoke, looks like an oil fire. Oil line to one of the bearings fractured under the vibration, I think."

"Never mind what you think," said Lukin flatly. "Emergency fire party will be on the way. And—" He hesitated, but couldn't see any alternative. "We'll reduce speed to fifteen kilometers and go up to periscope depth. That should reduce pressure on the glands enough to permit repairs. How are smoke conditions?"

The answer was a coughing spell, which told Lukin more than any words could have. "Very well. We'll raise the snorkel as soon as we're at periscope depth and put the ventilators on emergency. In the meantime, you are authorized to get into smoke gear."

"We're already putting it on," came back from the engine room. "And the machinist of the watch has isolated the ruptured oil line. He's cutting it out now."

"Well done, comrades," said Lukin. He meant it. That was fast work. In a smoke-fogged and spray-filled engine room, too. It reflected great credit on the engineering watch. Perhaps *Thunderbolt*'s crew was not such a weak point after all.

But then Lukin realized that this made no real difference. Undeniably, *Thunderbolt* had lost her race with the American submarine. On the control room sonar repeater, her echo was already opening the distance between the two ships. Lukin's rage and frustration fought a short, sharp battle with his common sense. He hated to admit defeat. But if he didn't take the strain off *Thunderbolt*, he would be facing not only defeat but disaster. Fire and flooding could conceivably destroy *Thunderbolt*, sending her down to the bottom a lifeless hulk. At the very least they could force her to surface, helpless and humiliated, exposed to the eyes of any ship or plane passing by. Those eyes would probably be Western. And then there would be a long, limping voyage or even a tow behind a Russian fishing trawler back home.

Admiral Barsukov would not be pleased.

There was no choice. Lukin sighed. "Reduce speed to fifteen kilometers," he said. "Take her up to periscope depth." He was conscious of all eyes in the control room on him as he spoke. He was further aware that the American would be watching—and probably gloating.


There was no mistaking the delight in Kitter's voice as it came over the intercom. "He's slowing way down and blowing his tanks, sir. He's giving up and going up!"

Cheever's eyes swung to the display cube. The sonar echo that was the Russian submarine was suddenly falling rapidly behind the racing *Devilfish*. And it was also creeping up toward the surface.

There was dead silence in the control room for another two minutes as everyone watched the display. By that time the Russian submarine was a good three miles farther behind and had risen nearly three hundred feet toward the surface.

Then the cheering began. It was against navy customs and regulations to congratulate or praise a superior, but the expressions on the faces of every man in the control room as they looked at John Cheever said all that was necessary. Frank Bronson's grin was so wide that it seemed to meet at the back of his head.

Cheever let his breath out in a long sigh of relief. It felt very good.

Then swiftly his mind began working again. "We'll hold this speed for another half hour, just to rub it in on our friend. We'll slow down when we start to lose sonar contact on him and go up to periscope depth. I want to send off a message on this little—fracas. We may also need to help our friend, or at least call in somebody else to help him. Preferably somebody from our side."

Bronson's grin flickered again. "That would sort of put the cherry on the sundae for our friend, wouldn't it, sir?"

"It would," said Cheever. "But he may not need anything except a few emergency repairs that he can make himself. And of course I'm sure he'll want to send off a report too." He took a deep breath to get rid of the last traces of tension.

"If he turns out to be shipshape and Bristol fashion after a few hours, we'll head back in toward him and see if he wants to play again. If he doesn't, he doesn't. But if he does—well, as far as I'm concerned, he can stay with us as long as he wants to. If he wants to follow us around—" He left the sentence unfinished.

"Where are we going to lead him, sir?" said Nielsen.

"One piece of deep ocean is much like another," said Cheever. "But if we decide we want to go someplace in particular, I think we'll head for Saint Helena, down in the South Atlantic."

"Good God," said Nielsen. "That's damned near three thousand miles!"

"I know. Nearly a week's cruising unless we hurry. If

our friend follows us that far, we can be pretty sure he's really eager. Then we can think of doing something—more—to entertain him. Anybody who wants to think of what we can do—go ahead. We've got plenty of time."

He turned to the officer of the watch. "Course 140. Maintain speed and depth."

## 18

Sonar conditions were particularly good. It was nearly three-quarters of an hour before Kitter reported that the Russian submarine's echo was beginning to fade.

"Slow to twenty-five knots," said Cheever. "Periscope depth."

*Devilfish* hydroplaned up from the depths, not blowing any ballast until she was barely two hundred feet down. As she neared the surface, Cheever ordered dead slow. *Devilfish*'s periscopes and surface sensors were housed in heavy steel tubes, but the pressure of the water at more than fifteen knots could bend the tubes and damage delicate lens mountings or circuitry.

*Devilfish* rose further until the depth gauge read sixty feet. "Hold her there," said Cheever, and scrambled up the ladder to the conning tower.

There he pressed a button. The periscope hummed up out of its well. Cheever bent to grab the handles and put his face against the padded eyepiece.

He saw the dark water rushing past. Then foam

tumbled around the lens as it broke surface. A moment later Cheever saw darkening blue sky flecked with clouds and blue-gray waves flecked with foam. It looked as though a good stiff wind was blowing up on the surface. But sixty feet down, *Devilfish* slid along as smoothly as if she were running on rails.

Cheever walked the periscope around, scanning the horizon in a complete 360-degree circle. Then he raised the radar and repeated the scan with that. When he was sure that the horizon was clear to the limits of both human and radar vision, he pressed one more button on the periscope mounting. The radio antenna poked itself up out of the sea behind the periscope.

"Transmit."

The pretaped message fled through the scrambler, up the antennae, then out at the speed of light to a naval communications satellite three thousand miles above. By the time it had reached the navy receiver in the United States, Cheever was lowering periscope, antenna, and radar mast. By the time it had been unscrambled, decoded, and rushed to Admiral Cappel, *Devilfish* was back in the deep sea again, heading back toward where she had left the Russian behind.

Admiral Cappel read the message over several more times until he was sure that he had it committed to memory. Then he opened the flap of the confidential waste disposal by his desk and dropped the yellow message flimsy into the hole. He leaned back in his chair and contemplated the situation. He also contemplated pouring himself a drink but decided against it.

So Johnny Cheever was planning on squaring off with *Devilfish* in a bout with a late-model Russian submarine. Or at least he would if the Russian was still willing to play—and if Cappel didn't have any objections. Cheever hadn't put that last point in the message; he hadn't needed to. His deference to Cappel's authority was always clear, but almost always unstated as well. Cappel returned the compliment by giving Cheever all the discretion he thought the younger man could handle.

But this was a ticklish matter. Should he let Johnny go ahead on the planned duel with the Russian submarine? He had authorized things like this before, although admittedly none that might stretch over three or four thousand miles and a week or ten days.

But there was more that set this duel apart from the others besides matters of time and distance. *Devilfish* was the single most valuable ship in the United States Navy. She was not expendable. On that point Cappel saw eye-to-eye with the most anti-Pentagon Congressional pennypincher who ever rose to make a speech, and he would admit as much.

But he didn't need to look over Johnny's shoulder on this point. Cheever knew the value of his ship as well as anybody and better than most. If it came to a choice between risking embarrassment and risking *Devilfish*, Cheever would do exactly the right thing at exactly the right moment.

There was McNeil, of course. The big scientist had made more than a few scathing remarks about "war games" and "tin sailors." He didn't care for the military side of O.S.S.O.'s workings and didn't mind who knew it. Cappel only hoped the CIA at least didn't know it. The agency was full of people who jumped to conclusions, and if they jumped to any conclusions about McNeil—

Cappel realized that his mind was wandering. It had been a long day, and the message that had come at the end of it hadn't helped matters. He sighed. As much as he tried to deny it to himself and others, he was getting old.

But back to McNeil. If *Devilfish*'s duel with the Russian involved any interference with the processor's operations, McNeil would be unhappy. And he would say so, long and loud, to the first person who happened to be handy. That, unfortunately, would be Johnny Cheever. McNeil might not make trouble, but if he did, Cheever would be the man stuck with it. So Cappel decided to forget about the scientist for the time being.

He couldn't do the same with the Russian submarine. It looked as though it had been on a specific mission. Whether that mission was to track *Devilfish* or not it was too soon to tell. But Johnny Cheever would be finding out in a few more hours and passing the word a few hours after that.

If the Russian did sit down on *Devilfish's* track, the next question was: what were his orders? The Russians very seldom played too rough if they thought there was any chance of their being caught. And in this case there was. *Devilfish* had sent out a message. It would be hard to arrange an "accident" that wouldn't look suspicious.

But that still didn't rule out the possibility. The Russians were obviously willing to play pretty damned rough where O.S.S.O. was concerned. The snatches had shown that. If there was somebody sufficiently iron-assed as honcho of the Russian side of this show—

Cappel sighed. There wasn't much he could do sitting here on shore. But one thing he could do was draft a message to *Devilfish*:

Evergreen State to Principal. Top secret captain's eyes only. Proceed with operations outlined in your message of 2237 today.

Johnny Cheever didn't need a direct order to go ahead and play games with the Russian. He would know what to do if Cappel said nothing. But if something went wrong, and politicians like Bergen started

134

raising a ruckus, it might help if Cheever could prove he had been acting under direct orders. It might help save his career, something that Cappel no longer had to worry about for himself.

Once the message was on its way, Cappel did open the desk drawer and break out the Irish whiskey. Two fingers only, however. It had been a long day. Between *Devilfish*'s situation and the search for Connie's murderers, it was going to be a long week.

The message from *Thunderbolt* stared at Admiral Barsukov from the polished top of his desk. Captain Volynsky stared at him from the other side of the desk. He did not much care for the looks of either one.

But one thing stood out. It was beginning to seem likely that *Thunderbolt* had found what she had been sent out to find. An American submarine that could match *Thunderbolt*'s speed to the limit and then pull away from her after her own machinery began to give under the strain—

Volynsky seemed to have read his thoughts. "It could be *Devilfish*, Comrade Admiral." Then he threw cold water on the idea, saying, "Or it could simply be a late-model American nuclear attack submarine. They are constantly making improvements, even within existing classes. There is also a new attack class supposed to be coming into service. So there are a good many possibilities besides *Devilfish*."

Barsukov's answer was a growl. He clasped his right hand—the real one—over the steel claw on his left arm, and lowered his massive chin onto his chest as he considered the situation.

After a moment he raised his head, realizing that there was in fact nothing to consider. All they could do with the information they had was to guess. Barsukov hated guesswork.

*Thunderbolt* would have to stay on the trail of the

American submarine that had so obligingly remained in the area. Why? Barsukov had a sudden, chilling moment of wondering if the American were playing the cat to *Thunderbolt*'s mouse.

But there was no alternative. He would have to send the orders to Lukin. And that meant increased risk for him. If *Thunderbolt* had sunk or broken down during the chase carried out by Lukin on his own, the responsibility would have been the little commander's. But now Barsukov was issuing an order. Blame for anything that happened could be laid at his door. And it would be. He was sure of that.

## 19

Two days went by. Out in the Atlantic, the two submarines slid steadily south at twenty-five knots, a thousand feet down. Neither one was ever off the other's sonar or out of the mind of the other's captain. Both crews came to accept the presence of the other submarine, much as they accepted the pressure of the sea on the hulls of their ships.

But the two captains could not passively relax and take the situation for granted. Lukin was becoming more and more certain that he was indeed trailing *Devilfish*. The shape the submarine ahead showed on the sonar and the sound her propellers and internal machinery made were unlike those of any other submarine. Every twelve hours he rose to periscope depth to send a report to Admiral Barsukov. At least that often he received a ULF transmission from the admiral. Lukin's reports never changed, and neither did Barsukov's orders. The chase went on.

Cheever did not have to worry about orders from home or reporting. But a message torpedo was kept ready to launch, and the tape-recorded log of the chase in it was updated every time the watch changed. If something went permanently wrong—through acts of God or acts of the submarine behind them—Cappel would get a complete report of everything that had happened up to that moment. There was no danger of *Devilfish's* disappearing mysteriously, which was as much as you could expect with a submarine.

Of course, if the Russian did swing and missed— well, SOP as far as Cappel's standing orders were concerned was to swing back. But that wasn't something to worry about in advance. Cheever kept a number of contingency plans for retaliation in mind and discussed them with Frank Bronson.

He also kept a weather eye on Doctor McNeil. The scientist was obviously on edge, and so were his technicians. But so far none of them showed any real instability. All of them were doing their jobs, and so— more or less—was the processor.

The second batch from the processor was still unwelcome in O'Hara's galley. And it wasn't exactly welcome on the plates of the crew, either. But the flavor, though powerful, was no longer completely nauseating, and the consistency resembled nothing worse than oatmeal. To set a good example, the wardroom made two complete meals off batch two.

It was obvious that eating the output of the processor was not only an important experiment; it was a cheap way of keeping Doctor McNeil happy. The scientist was finding most of his relief from the tension of the situation in keeping watch over the processor and its products. If having people eat them with a smile was good for Doctor McNeil—well, that was one less thing to worry about.

In fact, there wasn't much for Cheever to do at all, except routine paperwork and trying to keep away from the galley when O'Hara ran off a fresh batch of Danish pastry. But he did have at least one other thing to wonder about—how Admiral Cappel was doing, holding down the shoreside end of Operation Endless Voyage.

Admiral Cappel spent the first two days sweating through a particularly monumental Washington heat wave. On the third day he had lunch with David Wilton, the FBI agent, at a Chinese restaurant in Georgetown. Both men made sure they were not being tailed, and both carried concealed scrambler devices to guard against bugged martinis. It was Wilton who suggested these precautions, but Cappel willingly agreed to them. From his experience with Wilton, this suggested the man was on to something hot.

"Okay, David," the admiral said over the won-ton soup. "What have you got?"

"We've traced the Buick. It belonged to—well, never mind the name. They live over on the eastern shore about thirty miles south of your Complex One. And the car was reported stolen only about four hours before the snatch on Ms. Gilman."

Cappel knew that something important lay hidden in that fact, but his experience in intelligence work wasn't enough to make him sure what. So he waited until Wilton took his silence as a cue to go on.

"It looks remarkably as though the snatch was set up on fairly short notice—taking advantage of an opportunity that came up suddenly."

"Does that narrow things down—looking for the leak?"

138

"Is the Pope a Catholic? It certainly does narrow it down. From about ten days to—at a guess, less than twenty-four hours."

"Guess?"

"I'm necessarily going somewhat by my experience of cases like this in the past. Appearances could be deceiving, but—" Wilton hesitated, then fell silent. Cappel knew that David's silences were not a cue for him to say anything to prompt the agent. When David Wilton fell silent in the middle of a conversation, it usually meant that he was about to describe a hair-raisingly delicate situation.

"Admiral," said Wilton finally. "Is Peter Langer ready to be interrogated yet?"

"As a matter of fact, the doctor called last night. He said he'd let—someone—talk to him tomorrow."

"Good," said Wilton explosively. "Admiral—did you have anyone in particular in mind?"

"I was thinking you might—" Cappel broke off as he saw the FBI man shaking his head. "Why not?"

Wilton kept his voice low. "I've been doing some examination of files. Do you know that Ms. Gilman nearly got down-checked as a security risk because of her association with Peter Langer?"

"No, I didn't." Cappel kept his voice low also, but with an effort. So the damned game of spy and counterspy had reached out to his office! He wasn't surprised. But he was angry.

"There's a solid record on him from the 60's campus radical organizations, the works. Nothing to suggest that he himself has any subversive beliefs. But it's good odds that he's got at least one friend who's tied in with the Russians, either willingly or under pressure. And he himself is likely to balk at talking to the FBI."

"Why should he? If Russian agents murdered his fiancée—"

"But he's the type who won't believe they were Rus-

139

sian agents. He'll get very much on edge and on guard. If he does, it will take weeks to break him down. I don't want to take that kind of time. And he may decide to blab to the papers. We won't even be able to get near him after that, let alone get him to talk. And Senator Bergen will have fun.

"Besides, even if Langer doesn't talk to the papers, we may find ourselves in hot water from another source. The CIA has a file on Langer and they're in position to move in on him any time they want to."

"Oh, hell," said Cappel. "What do they want with him?"

"The same thing we want—information that they can use to trace the leak from O.S.S.O. But you know how the CIA's field men tend to be when they're working domestically."

Cappel did. The CIA earned a good part of its keep when it worked abroad. But its operations in the United States were not only illegal; they were often—to put it politely—rather heavy-handed.

The expression on his face was the answer Wilton was apparently looking for. "Exactly. If Langer doesn't talk—and he won't—they'll do their best to pin something on him. That way they can hope to look good even if the Russians get away. But all they'll really do is blow the whole case wide open. There will be no damned way on earth of keeping it out of the papers. Bergen will have us all roasted for cocktail snacks."

"How close are they to moving in on Langer?"

"They've got two people that we know about permanently on the staff of the secure ward at Bethesda. What they can call up if they want to move—I don't know. But I hope we can move before they do. I can't do anything, and neither can anybody else from the FBI. Not without pushing the CIA into moving. The CIA doesn't like us, they haven't since J. Edgar

140

Hoover's day, and they probably won't for another twenty years."

Wilton looked at the admiral. "I know it's asking you to step outside your normal responsibilities and take an extra risk. But—would you be willing to talk to Peter Langer?"

Cappel looked back at the FBI man. He had seen this coming some time back. His opinion of inter-agency spy politics had always been low. It wasn't any higher now, as much as he respected David Wilton. It took more than friendship and trust for the agent to make him happy about playing the essentially dirty game.

But he would play. It offered a considerable chance of helping O.S.S.O., for which he would willingly do a good deal more than just talk to one mixed-up young man. And if things blew—well, he was the most expendable man in the office, when all was said and done.

"All right, Dave," said Cappel. "I'll go in tomorrow."

Somewhat to his surprise, neither the tension nor the hot weather gave Cappel a sleepless night. His old ability to keep calm under unlikely circumstances was reasserting itself. That at least was good news.

So he looked and felt fit and confident the next morning. He was ready to be either gentle and polite or loud and threatening, depending on what he felt Peter Langer required. But he was careful to dress in his oldest and least uniform-like civilian suit.

The nurse at Bethesda let him in to see Peter immediately after breakfast. The young man still looked like death warmed over, but he was sitting up in bed and his pale face was alert. He even managed a strained smile to greet the admiral.

"You must be Admiral Cappel," he said. His voice

was distorted by the partial cast on his lower jaw, but recognizable. "Connie"—there was a catch in his voice as he said the name—"Connie described you several times. She—rather liked you, you know."

"I rather liked her too," said Cappel quietly. "That's one of the reasons I came over to see you."

"Why is that?" Cappel noted that Peter's voice was uncertain, but not yet suspicious. He decided to go on in a low key.

"Because we have some leads on the people we believe killed her. I think you can help us follow them up."

Peter's face and voice did become wary this time. "What do you mean?"

"I mean that Connie was murdered by Russian agents. Kidnapped, probably tortured, certainly drugged, then murdered." No point in not being blunt.

For a moment Cappel thought he had perhaps been too blunt. Peter's battered face hardened. "I don't want to listen to spy stories. You military types are always seeing things."

Cappel let the slap pass by without comment. But he also let his own face and voice harden slightly. "Peter, I'm not telling you any spy stories. We are as sure of this as we can be."

"Who's 'we,' Admiral? The FBI? The CIA? If you think I'm going to cooperate with that bunch of Fascists, you—"

Cappel decided to push matters. He rose. "No, I guess you're not. I guess you don't want to help us catch Connie's murderers, either. If you feel that way about it, there's nothing we can do." He turned toward the door.

He had his hand on the knob when he heard Peter clear his throat. "Uh—wait a minute, Admiral Cappel. I—did the Russians really—?"

Cappel turned. "If I told you one hundred percent

'yes' I would be telling you a lie. But I can tell you the truth if I say we're *almost* certain. There were drugs in Connie's body that nobody except Russian intelligence uses." Some of them were also popular with the CIA and the British MI5, but this wasn't the time to mention that detail.

"Okay," said Peter. "But I don't see what I can do for you. I've already given you the license number. I didn't see any of the men's faces or anything like that."

"No," said Cappel. He couldn't help tensing up inside. Here was the ticklish point. "But we believe that the murder was planned very hastily by somebody who had learned that you were planning to pick Connie up at Complex One."

"How could they learn that? I—oh—" The "oh" came out in a very small voice.

"Exactly. Who knew what you were planning for that evening? And how?"

"Who—who did I talk to, in other words?" Peter's voice seemed to be hanging between defiance and guilt.

"That's about it."

Peter hesitated. Cappel tried not to stare too hard at the pale face with the plaster-encased jaw and the bandaged nose—and the trembling lip.

"You're asking me to get my friends in trouble, Admiral. I don't—I don't want to—"

Cappel decided it was safe to interrupt. He kept his voice low but made it cool and sharp. It was time to drive the matter home.

"Peter, one of those friends may have gotten Connie murdered in a very horrible way, and nearly got you killed as well. I'm not saying he did it deliberately. But the Russians are always on the lookout for information about the movements of people they're after. It's a hell of a thing to do, but it's a hell of a world we live in."

The admiral hesitated before going on. He might be pushing matters too far by saying this, but— "And it may not have been an accident. You may have among your friends somebody who's working for Russian intelligence. Possibly they're being blackmailed, possibly they're doing it freely. That's not important. But that 'friend' may have murdered Connie Gilman just as if he'd put the pistol to her head and pulled the trigger himself."

Fortunately, that was all Cappel had planned to say, because at that point he noticed that Peter was crying. Silently, and obviously trying hard to hide it. But the tears were about to brim over.

Cappel stood up again and headed for the door. He didn't think Peter needed—or could take—any more. Not now.

At the door he turned and said quietly, "Peter. Think it over. The nurse has all my phone numbers. When you feel like it, call me. Give me—whatever you want to give—and it won't go any farther than necessary." He went out and closed the door softly behind him.

The message was waiting for Cappel by the time he got back to his Pentagon office. He returned Peter's call, listened briefly, then thanked the young man and hung up. He wished he could thank Peter in person. He deserved it, considering how much it was obviously costing him.

But Cappel had other calls to make first. He began with one to the White House. He had known the President when the other was a junior Congressman and one of the early supporters of atomic submarines. They were not exactly friends, but the President knew and respected Cappel's judgment. And he would back up the admiral when the chips were down.

Then he called David Wilton.

"Hello, Dave. I've got a name for you."

"Just one?"

"Just one. Charles Pender."

"Charles Pender." A long silence. "I'll be damned. The Charles Pender?"

"Yes. Senator Bergen's administrative assistant."

## 20

Several more days passed. Admiral Cappel went back to his paperwork, waiting for a call from David Wilton. The call did not come, but Admiral Cappel was not bothered by that. He and the FBI agent had agreed not to see each other or even talk to each other until Wilton had some hard evidence. And even David Wilton could not produce hard evidence as easily as a magician pulling rabbits and colored silk flags out of a hat.

But he also knew that he would be very happy if Wilton did turn up something hard against Charles Pender. It seemed almost too good to be true, that he had the chance of striking a blow against Connie's murderers and Senator Bergen at the same time. In fact, it probably was too good to be true. Something would go wrong to keep things from working out so neatly. But Cappel had seen enough plans fall apart to be used to the possibility.

Meanwhile, the two submarines continued their deep-sea game of follow-the-leader. Even the two captains were beginning to have to fight to stay alert and ready for an unexpected move by the other side. But both were helped by the suspicion that something would happen when they reached St. Helena.

Cheever was in his cabin talking with Frank Bronson.

"The British don't normally keep any naval forces permanently assigned to the island," he said. "Warships sometimes call on their way around the Cape of Good Hope, and also survey vessels. Passenger-cargo ships from the Union-Castle Line stop by once a month, but they don't carry any sonar or listening gear or experienced soundmen. If one of them picked us up, it would be pure luck on his part and sloppiness on ours."

Bronson nodded. "Let's go back to worrying about our friend back there." He pointed toward the stern. "I gather you want to lead him in as close to the island as possible."

"I do. I'd like to get in close enough so that we can bottom at free-diving depth. St. Helena's an undersea mountain, so its approaches are very steep. We'll have to get well in before we can bottom in under three hundred feet."

Bronson was silent for a moment. Then his face split in a particularly wolfish grin. "You've got something on your mind, sir—haven't you? Something nasty."

"I hope our Russian friend will think it's nasty. Not fatal, but nasty."

The intercom beeeeped. "Sound room, sir. Our friend is going up to periscope depth again."

"Sounds like he's sending another message," said Bronson.

"Probably," said Cheever. "I'd give a good deal to know how much he's guessed about us and how accurate it is."

*Thunderbolt's* depth gauge swung past twenty meters, then steadied. The periscope slid up out of the well and thrust upward through the water. Foam tumbled in front of it; then gray sea and gray sky showed, bare and empty. No ships, no planes, not even a seagull or a broaching whale.

Lukin nodded and the radio antenna shot up beside the periscope. The pretaped message with a recording of the American submarine's propeller noises went racing out into space, to be relayed homeward by satellite.

The message also contained Lukin's estimate of the situation. The American was heading straight for St. Helena, now only five hours away at their present speed. He showed no sign of altering course. If the American proceeded into British territorial waters—and here Lukin had hesitated before asking—should *Thunderbolt* follow?

He had hesitated because he wasn't sure if Admiral Barsukov would give him a clear answer. Barsukov obviously wanted the American—*Devilfish*—dealt with as drastically as possible. But would he be prepared to take the responsibility for drastic action off Lukin's shoulders?

Cheever and Bronson had moved now from Cheever's cramped cabin to the temporarily empty wardroom. The wardroom was no larger than the dining room of a small house, but it was a little less claustrophobic than the cabin.

Over coffee and some of O'Hara's doughnuts, they were thrashing out their plans for dealing with the Russian submarine. Cheever finally shoved his plate and cup aside and said, "I'd also like to drop the deep diver and have it do a quick survey for a bottoming site. St. Helena's all rock, and I don't want to risk damaging the propellers or torpedo launchers."

"No indeed," said Bronson. "But with Rabinowitz

147

out, we've only got one qualified deep diver operator besides me. That's Fishman. We don't have much backup if Fishman has a tough job."

"You're forgetting something, Frank," said Cheever. "We've got the designer of the deep diver aboard too."

"Doctor McNeil?" Bronson sounded skeptical almost to the point of questioning Cheever's sanity. "Do you really think—?"

"I wouldn't be proposing it if I didn't think McNeil could handle the job," said Cheever. "At least I intend to ask him. I'd say most of his trouble in the past week has been not having anything to do. At least, not having anything to do that the rest of us think is useful," he added. "He is obviously very much on the defensive with the crew. That's adding to the strain and making him feel even worse than he would otherwise."

"But if he's that edgy, do you think he can safely operate a deep diver on what might turn out to be a hairy one? Suppose the Russian starts tracking the deep diver and decides to try for an easy kill?"

"We'll send Nielsen along with McNeil as crew. If it looks like something's going to happen that McNeil can't handle, he'll have orders to take over."

"All right, sir," said Bronson. "Should I call McNeil?"

"Yes. We're only about four hours out now, and I want to give him time to refresh his memory on a deep diver's controls after I brief him."

"Aye aye, sir."

This time Admiral Barsukov was giving all his attention to the message on his desk and none of it to Captain Volynsky. Commander Lukin was asking for advice and permission. This had happened before, since there were limits to the little commander's arrogant self-confidence. But Barsukov wasn't sure what Lukin's motives were now, and he didn't like the ones he suspected.

Lukin wanted to go into action against the American submarine—against *Devilfish*. That was obvious. But it was equally obvious that he wanted any initiative he might take to be covered by an order from Barsukov. That way, if something went wrong and the higher-ups started looking for a head to put in the noose, it would more likely be Barsukov's than Lukin's.

Barsukov raised his eyes to the fat man across the desk from him, then raised them further to look out the window. Volynsky would be no help in this situation. Neither would anybody else who had never taken a submarine out to sea and grappled with an enemy far below the waves, wondering if you would ever see the sun again and trying to shut the doubts out of your mind.

It was up to him.

Barsukov's eyes fell to the message again. This was *Devilfish*. In his own mind there was no longer any doubt about it, whatever anyone else felt. *Devilfish* was too valuable to let get away if there was any chance of doing something against her. It looked as though that chance might be coming up within the next few hours.

When it was broken down into those elements, the problem no longer seemed to exist. Barsukov knew what he had to do and what he had to order. He looked at Captain Volynsky.

"I am going to order Lukin to move against *Devilfish* to the most extreme limit."

"If he thinks he can escape detection," put in the captain. "They are very close to St. Helena. If *Thunderbolt* takes action that the British can detect—"

"Their forces in the area are negligible," said Barsukov with a wave of his claw-hand. "The only thing to worry about is the Americans." He glared at the fat captain. Trust a man who had spent his whole career

149

in offices instead of control rooms to start getting nervous when the situation suddenly became dangerous. Oh, well, there was nothing he could do about Volynsky. His career had made him what he was, and there was no hope of changing him this late in life.

In fact, it might be worthwhile to try a peace overture. "Comrade Captain," he said. "Would you care for a game of chess?"

Volynsky's ponderous head nodded, making his triple chins quiver. Barsukov opened the bottom left-hand drawer of his desk and pulled out the board and pieces. He took out a black and a white pawn, closed a hand around each one, and held out both claw and natural hand to Volynsky.

"Make your choice, Comrade Captain."

Doctor McNeil found Cheever's cabin a tight fit unless he stood and leaned back against the door. Cheever suspected that McNeil was also standing because it let him look down on the captain. But the big scientist was obviously none too happy with his situation. Cheever would let him have whatever psychological props he might feel he needed.

Cheever had decided to be blunt, and he knew he had to be quick. "Doctor McNeil. Have you kept up your qualifications on the deep diver Mark II?"

McNeil laughed shortly. "I designed the minisub, Captain. I damned well ought to."

"That's not quite what I asked, Doctor. Can you operate one on a mission—say, in about three hours?"

There was a long silence in the cabin. Cheever saw the scientist's face working in doubt and confusion over what lay behind the question. He wondered what other emotions were lurking behind the massively boned dark face.

"Why, Captain?" said McNeil. He seemed oddly subdued.

Cheever went rapidly over the situation they were facing, up to the point of describing the need for a quick survey of the bottom. He didn't care to discuss the rest of his plans, remembering some of the things McNeil had said about "war games."

"Give me an hour to get the layout of the controls back in my mind," said McNeil, "and I'll take her anywhere. But"—he hesitated—"are you—doing me a favor—with this?"

Cheever would have liked to be able to answer swiftly, briskly, decisively. But this time he had to weigh his words. Was McNeil honestly curious, or was he looking for some imagined slight?

Well, there was only one possible answer to give, whatever the effect might be.

"No, Doctor, I'm not doing you a favor." Cheever smiled. "I don't do people favors with expensive equipment like a Mark II deep diver. It's just that you happen to be the best man available for the job." That was very definitely a white lie. Both Bronson and Fishman Nielsen were probably as good at the controls of a deep diver as McNeil. But if McNeil was good enough, and if doing the job was good for him—

White lie or not, the answer was the right one. McNeil smiled, a smile that was frank, open, and not nervous at all. "Thanks, Captain. I'd like to do something, but I'll be damned if I'm going to take any favors. Too damned many—" He appeared to think the better of going on and broke off suddenly. Then he smiled again. "Incidentally, there's going to be another batch out of the processor in about twelve hours. I think it's going to be a considerable improvement over what we've done."

"Frankly, Doctor, I hope so. But forget about the processor for the time being. For about the next eight hours, keep your mind on our deep diver and the underwater approaches to St. Helena."

151

Commander Lukin was conferring with the chief diver in his cabin for privacy's sake. It was imperative that as few men as possible know as little as possible about what was going to happen to *Devilfish*.

"After the detailed examination, place the limpet mines. Place them near the bow. That will produce maximum flooding and the least interference with the mines' sonar receivers. We also want to reduce the risk of rupturing the pressure vessel of *Devilfish's* reactor and causing a detectable radioactive leak."

"I understand, Comrade Captain."

"As soon as *Devilfish* gets underway, we will proceed on her trail again. When we are at least one hundred kilometers clear of St. Helena, we will command-detonate the mines. *Devilfish* will go down, on the high seas, with all hands and in water much too deep for salvage. Or so the Americans will think. But she will have gone down in a location precisely known to us. Our oceanographic vessels are extremely well equipped, and they will take care of the rest."

"It would be an even greater victory to capture her, Comrade Captain."

"No doubt. It would also be a great event if the Volga River turned to vodka. But neither event is very likely. Destroying *Devilfish* will make the Americans very unhappy and will teach us a good deal. That is enough of a victory for the moment."

"Yes, Comrade Captain."

Each working on his own plans, the two captains drove their ships on toward the island ahead.

## 21

There was silence outside in the sea and silence inside the deep diver as it glided toward the rocky shelf on the submerged slopes of St. Helena. In the front seat, Doctor McNeil raised his eyes from the controls for a moment and looked back at the telephone cable. It writhed away into the darkness that hid *Devilfish* three miles behind. Then quickly he turned back to the controls and the delicate act of balancing the deep diver on its hydrojets against the currents flowing along the rocky slopes.

This was a delicate job, even in a conventional research deep diver. But the navy had taken McNeil's brainchild and fitted it with extra weaponry and equipment that altered its weights and balances. McNeil needed all his skill and experience to keep ahead of the little submarine.

The weapons and related gear were the responsibility of Fishman Nielsen, who sat in the second seat, his bearded face dimly reflected in McNeil's viewports. For the moment Nielsen had nothing to do but monitor a sonar screen that showed nothing but the solid echo of *Devilfish*. The Russian submarine was still out there, but it was beyond the range of the deep diver's small sonar set. Both men in the minisub hoped they also were out of reach of the Russian's sonar, screened by *Devilfish*'s much larger and noisier mass. Cheever was maneuvering the big submarine as delicately as a Japanese artist doing brushwork, using the bow thruster and screws in ever-changing combinations.

A voice sounded in McNeil's earphones. It was Frank Bronson, acting as communicator between the two submarines. "Deep diver. The Russian has just gone to dead slow. He's still eight hundred feet down, but he's altering course slightly. It looks like he's planning to stay well offshore until he's sure what we're doing. Got us a bottom site yet?"

McNeil scanned the bottom contour the sonar was inscribing on a roll of paper, then visually doublechecked out the ports. "We may be coming up on one right now. Hold on for a second." McNeil opened the throttle a little more, speeding up the hydrojets' impellers. The submarine's speed shot up from two to nearly four knots. McNeil flicked his eyes back and forth from the fathometer to the viewports. Silence stretched from one minute into two, then into a third as McNeil doubled back to get a clear notion of the size of the level patch in the rocky slope.

The fourth minute was half gone when he got on the telephone. "Devilfish, we're right in the middle of an area that should do. Come in at about"—he checked the depth gauge—"250 feet; then float down directly. The surface is rugged, but fairly level, and it's large enough."

"Four-oh," said Bronson. "We'll go in bow first and bottom with a slight down-angle on the bow. That should keep the screws out of the rocks. You people hold position until we've closed to one hundred yards; then clear the area to port. That will keep you screened from our friend until the last minute."

"Aye aye," said McNeil. His hands and eyes moved back to the controls, and he eased the deep diver almost to a stop in the water. Behind them, Devilfish began to grow on the sonar screen.

"The American is definitely on the bottom, at ninety-six meters," said the soundman's voice in Commander Lukin's ears.

"Very good, Comrade," said Lukin briskly. "Keep a passive listening watch for the moment. Do not begin echo-ranging unless he starts his engines."

"Yes, Comrade Captain."

Lukin switched circuits on the intercom. "Comrade Lieutenant, are your men ready?"

The voice of the chief diver replied from the airlock compartment aft. "All ready, Comrade Captain."

"Very good. We are going to rise to one hundred meters and let you out. You will rig your torpedo to the towing bollard and run the tow line out to two hundred meters. We will then move in at minimum speed to a range of two thousand meters. At that point you will cast off, close the rest of the way under the torpedo's power, and proceed as previously ordered. Is that clear?"

"It is, Comrade Captain."

"Good. Then—I wish you good luck and a part in our great victory."

Lukin could not quite manage to wish them a safe return. When all was said and done, the divers were expendable. If there was any conflict between their safety and *Thunderbolt*'s, the four divers would never see home again.

But Lukin could see no good reason why this conflict should arise. The American submarine was being as cooperative as if her captain had received orders from the Pentagon to play sitting duck for *Thunderbolt*. Lukin had expected ten to twenty hours of nerve-wracking, slow-speed maneuvering around the underwater cliffs of St. Helena before the American tried going quietly down onto the bottom. But instead, *Devilfish* had gone straight for a level spot on the slopes like a lost lamb for its mother. Most interesting.

And most fatal. *Thunderbolt* would tow her divers in most of the way, saving their strength. The bulk of her hull and the turbulence in the wake of her propeller would screen them and their little electric riding torpedo from American sonar and listening gear.

But Lukin could not entirely suppress a nagging doubt. There was no sense in the American going to the bottom when he must know he was within sonar range of *Thunderbolt*, and his location would be instantly revealed. Did he have some plan of his own that involved this odd tactic? Or did he perhaps hope that he was actually out of *Thunderbolt's* detection range?

Yes, that must be it. The American was deluding himself. With that settled in his own mind, Lukin found that he could breathe easier.


"Our friend's still coming straight in," came Bronson's voice on the telephone. "It almost looks as though he wants to ram his bow up between our propellers."

"Rather vulgar of him," said McNeil. The light tone covered nerves that were gradually being stretched tighter and tighter. They did not conceal the sweat that was breaking out all over him. He felt it prickling and starting to run under the wetsuit. Both he and Nielsen were wearing scuba gear, although the deep diver was sealed and pressurized. But Cheever had warned them to be ready for "a little swim, just in case."

It was beginning to look as if they might be taking that little swim. The Russian couldn't be planning on moving in and destroying *Devilfish* here in British territorial waters. Or could her captain be just mad enough for that? At least the two men in the deep diver might be safe enough if they lay doggo where

156

they were until the Russian was gone. But they would watch and hear *Devilfish* die, knowing that all the men aboard her were being pulped by in-rushing water, their blood spreading in clouds—

With a terrible effort of self-control McNeil clamped down on the pictures racing through his mind. He took several deep breaths and stared off into space for a long moment until he was sure that his voice would be steady. Then he looked at the sonar screen—and looked a second and a third time.

The Russian submarine had closed to within four thousand yards of *Devilfish*. She was slightly farther from the deep diver, which lay five hundred yards off to port of *Devilfish*, but still within easy range of the minisub's sonar. The enormous echo of the slowly closing Russian submarine loomed large on the dark glass of the screen in front of McNeil.

But the deep diver's sonar also showed a smaller echo behind the Russian submarine, where nothing of the kind should be. It was about two hundred yards behind, holding distance and depth steadily, as if it were tied to the submarine.

McNeil's mouth opened as a thought suddenly struck him. Maybe it was.

"*Devilfish*, we're picking up a small echo holding steady about two hundred yards dead astern of the Russian. Do you have anything?"

"Negative, deep diver. He's coming at us bows-on and anything astern of him is going to be screened from us by his hull. What does the echo look like?"

McNeil turned his eyes back to the sonar screen. The echo was still there, as enigmatic as ever. "I honestly can't say it's anything I've ever seen before. But it's holding the same speed and depth as the sub, and constant distance too. I wonder if it might be something he's towing in?" He didn't put in any ideas as to what the "something" might be. Bronson knew the range of possibilities much better than he did. Besides, too much thinking about this might get the nerves jumping again.

Again everyone was silent as the Russian submarine glided on toward Devilfish like a giant shark on the prowl.

"He's turning!" exploded both McNeil and Bronson in the same moment. Then Bronson went on swiftly, "He's swinging very hard to port, toward you. Do you still have that trailing echo?"

"Still got it," said McNeil. "And it's—no, wait a minute, it's beginning to open the distance and it's stopped matching depth. It's—no, it's just put on a burst of speed. It's catching up with the submarine and—oh shit, the echoes've merged. Can't separate the two any more." McNeil found his hands clutching the control wheel as though he wanted to bend the heavy steel and felt the sweat breaking out all over again.

"Never mind that," said Bronson, "We got a quick look at it when the Russian turned. You're right, it looked like something he was—"

"I've got it again!" shouted McNeil. "About two hundred feet depth, about a thousand yards on a bearing of 210. It's moving in toward the slope and—oh damn, lost it again. I think it's gone behind some rocks on the bottom."

"Nice work, Doctor," came a new voice on the line. It was Cheever himself. "Can you shift the deep diver around so it's bows-on to Devilfish without losing a 360-degree sonar coverage?"

McNeil did a quick scan of the sonar portrait of the bottom around him. "I think so, Captain."

"Good. Do it, but very quietly. Minimum power and don't get too high off the bottom. We don't want to give the Russians any hint you're out and around."

For the next two minutes McNeil was occupied in gently lifting the minisub off the bottom and repositioning it with its bow pointing toward *Devilfish*. He managed to do it without rising more than five feet off the bottom. There was an unmistakable look of respect in Nielsen's eyes by the time the deep diver settled back into place on the bottom.

"She's repositioned, Captain," said McNeil. "What now?"

"Doctor McNeil, I think we're moving into a combat situation. I'm going to ask you—do you want Chief Nielsen to take over the controls of the deep diver?"

The question wasn't exactly a surprise to McNeil. But he still didn't have a ready answer for it. Instead, he replied with a question of his own. "What sort of combat situation?"

"I think our Russian friend has dropped divers," was Cheever's reply. "I think he's planning to have them slip in from your side with limpet mines as a present for us. I want to make sure that present goes astray, but *silently*. If our friend's divers just quietly vanish—

"But that's getting ahead of things. The main point is that your deep diver is our best chance of pulling off what I have in mind. I want to use it against those divers when they come in. But when the shooting starts, Chief Nielsen might be better at the controls than you would be." Cheever's voice laid emphasis on the "might." "Do you want to give him the controls?"

McNeil was able to answer this time. "Captain, I don't *want* to. But—if you order me to—"

"I won't order you unless you honestly feel that you can't handle the sub—"

"When the shooting starts?" McNeil laughed harshly. "Thanks, Captain. But I've been sitting watching the processor, knowing that damned Russian sub was watching me for a week now. I not only think I can hack it—I damned well want to!"

There was an unusual silence on the line. Was John

Cheever actually *hesitating*? "All right, Doctor. Now, here's the plan—"

When the telephone conversation with the deep diver was over, Cheever flipped the switch, hung up the headset, and turned to Frank Bronson. The executive officer's face expressed the question that was too delicate to put into words.

"He'll do it," said Cheever, replying to the silent question.

"Sure?"

"He's got himself under control, and with luck it's not going to be that hard. Without luck—well, he's got Nielsen with him on the weapons board."

"Do you think it's fair to risk Fishman this way, sir?"

Cheever's voice had a slight edge when he replied. "Don't push it, Frank. Nielsen's not being 'risked' any more than he would be if he were doing it himself. Besides, McNeil's good enough with the deep diver for the job. I'm not throwing Fishman away to do good things for McNeil's head, if that's what you were thinking."

Bronson looked slightly shamefaced. Cheever slapped him on the shoulder. "Don't worry about it, Frank. But"—he paused for effect—"you might start routing your diving gear out of storage."

"Sir?"

"If we can bring off phase one of this little game, I want you to take care of phase two."

"When we return the compliment?"

"Right."

It was so quiet in the deep diver that the rumble of McNeil's stomach sounded as loud as the eruption of an undersea volcano. It reminded him that he had had no dinner. If those Russian divers delayed much longer, he was going to miss breakfast as well. No, wait.

160

He looked at his watch. Only ten minutes had passed since the last time he looked at it. Damn! He was really a hell of a lot more nervous than he had admitted to Cheever, or even than he had wanted to admit to himself. Was he just playing a game that he wouldn't be able to keep up if things really got rough? From the expression on Chief Nielsen's face, it was pretty obvious the other man was wondering about McNeil too.

And when would things get rough, if they did? They had been out here nearly an hour, waiting in ambush—and no sign of the Russians. The Russian sub had apparently bottomed somewhere between three and four miles off to port. Or at least she had gone off *Devilfish's* sonar at about that distance. Her divers were going to have a long swim back after doing whatever they were supposed to do to *Devilfish*.

With another vigorous effort at self-control, McNeil clamped down his mind's tendency to imagine one gruesome possibility after another. After all he had said about "war games," here he was playing quarterback in one of them, and he had *volunteered* for the job.

So if you want to play the stud, man, he told himself, play it *right*.

His eyes drifted back to the sonar screen. The minisub's sonar and listening gear were on their own now. At close ranges the minisub's sonar could track small targets better than *Devilfish's*, and with less danger of warning the enemy that they were being watched. The ranges would be very close this time. Cheever had said he expected the whole business to be done within five hundred yards of—

Unmistakably there was a moving echo on the edge of the screen.

McNeil heard Chief Nielsen draw his breath in with a hiss. But that was the only sound for nearly a minute, as they watched the echo acquire shape, direction, and distance. By the end of that minute it was easily recognizable as the same thing they had seen the Russian submarine dropping off. A small, wavering, blurry echo, consisting of four objects around a slightly larger one. The four Russian divers and their mount.

McNeil was on the phone in seconds after that. "Captain, we've got them on our screen. Bearing 190, depth 280, speed less than one knot. They look like they'll be right over us in another ten minutes. That means another five to seven minutes to you unless they speed up."

"They'll probably slow down," said Cheever. "All right, tell Chief Nielsen to man the external weapons-control panel. Be sure to flood the escape lock quietly, though. We don't want our friends to hear you."

McNeil almost laughed. That John Cheever was giving unnecessary advice about silence proved that even the iron-nerved captain wasn't quite as calm as he seemed. Good. McNeil had to admit that there had been times when he had been more afraid of the remote and duty-driven John Cheever than of the Russians.

He turned to Nielsen. "Chief, time to mount up."

"Aye aye, sir," said Nielsen. McNeil noted that it was the first time Fishman had ever said that to him as though he meant it. My God, thought McNeil—am I beginning to come across as a real officer? And a fighting man?

As McNeil considered that possibility, Chief Nielsen slipped into the airlock behind the passenger compartment. McNeil heard the squeak of a valve wheel being turned, then the hiss of escaping air and the faint burble of inrushing water. Nielsen was flooding the lock, until the pressure inside matched the pressure of the sea outside and he could open the external hatch. McNeil kept his eyes on the slowly approaching echo on the sonar. It gave no signs that any of the Russians had heard anything. Good.

162

A faint clunk as Nielsen opened the outer hatch, then over the intercom came his voice. "External weapons-control panel armed and ready, sir."

"Very good," said McNeil. He realized that his own tones were becoming as clipped and controlled as John Cheever's, and almost laughed at the notion.

The external weapons-control panel would have been no good if they had been planning to use any explosives against the Russians. A man in scuba gear at that panel would have been as vulnerable to underwater explosions as any of the Russians.

But they were going for a swift, silent kill now, and for that Chief Nielsen was better off outside. He could control deep diver's weapons as well, see better—and swim out much more quickly to strike the Russians down with his own pellet gun and knives if it came to that. McNeil was very glad he didn't have to worry about tackling that last job.

The Russians continued to close for the next five minutes. Then they briefly went off deep diver's sonar. McNeil had expected this—there was a blind angle directly overhead. But he practically held his breath until the echo reappeared. Now it was between the minisub and *Devilfish*.

From the silence on the telephone, McNeil suspected that John Cheever was also holding his breath.

The Russians were a hundred yards beyond the deep diver when McNeil inched open a ballast valve. Air flowed into a ballast tank, driving out three hundred pounds of water. It was enough to bring the minisub slowly up off the bottom but not enough to alert the Russians. They slipped silently on toward *Devilfish*.

They were halfway between the two American submarines when McNeil fed power from the batteries into the hydrojet. The deep diver began to move forward through the black waters until McNeil saw that they were overtaking the echo on their screen. Then he cut back the power. He didn't want to overtake the Russians too quickly. This was going to have to be very precisely timed.

A minute later the Russians stopped about one hundred yards from *Devilfish*. "Move in now?" McNeil asked Cheever.

"Not yet," said the captain. "I want them in much closer. Then I'm going to turn on the external lights—and good hunting."

A nasty thought occurred to McNeil. "What if that thing they're riding carries an armed charge and they just ram it home?"

"Then we get blown up," said Cheever calmly. "But the Russians don't normally go in for that sort of kamikaze mission. Trained divers are just as expensive for them as for us. Besides, they'll probably be under orders to observe as well as destroy."

McNeil hoped devoutly that Cheever wasn't being too charitable to the Russians.

A moment later the Russians' echo on the screen began to move again. McNeil reported it, then opened his throttle to half power. From outside sounded a series of clicks as Chief Nielsen armed the weapons panel.

Three hundred yards to *Devilfish*. Two-seventy. Two-fifty. The Russians had stopped again, about sixty yards out. Two-forty. Two-twenty. Would the Russians realize what was sneaking up behind them? Two hundred. The Russians still holding. McNeil opened the throttle wider. The closer deep diver got, the better the chance for a swift, silent kill.

One-eighty. One-sixty. One-fifty. The Russians still stationary. Were they holding a poker game? McNeil grinned and opened the throttle wider still. One-twenty. One hundred. Ninety. Eighty. The Russians were less than fifty feet away now—

And Cheever turned on the lights.

Instantly *Devilfish*'s two hundred and fifty feet were lit from stem to stern by a yellow glare that stripped away the blackness from the water and left it transparent blue-green. In that glare the four Russian divers on their torpedo seemed pinned and frozen, like insects trapped in crystal.

Before the Russians could recover from that surprise, Nielsen fired the two heavy harpoon launchers mounted on the deep diver. The finned titanium alloy rods they fired were designed for maximum weight and minimum cross-section. Fired from the heavy gas launchers, they could penetrate four inches of solid oak planking at fifty yards.

The bodies of the Russian divers were a great deal less tough than four inches of oak.

McNeil saw one Russian transfixed through both hips, the harpoon pinning him to the torpedo like a bug in a display case. The second harpoon slammed right through a second man's central air tank and through his body, bursting out of his chest. The man seemed to explode as high-pressure air blasted out of the ruptured tank, almost vanishing in a cloud of bubbles and blood.

Then the deep diver was surging up to the Russians, banging aside the fifteen-foot cylinder that was towing the divers. McNeil's mouth went dry as he wondered if the jar might set off an explosive charge. At least *Devilfish* would be safe if it did, but—

Then his hands were dancing assuredly over the control board. They were too close to the Russians to fire any more harpoons, but that didn't mean the deep diver was helpless. Both the Mark I and the Mark II were fitted with a pair of sophisticated clawlike mechanical arms. The claws were delicate enough to pick up an eggshell-fragile Greek vase from the bottom of the sea, strong enough to bend iron bars.

With a coolness that surprised him, McNeil manipulated the controls so that one claw reached out and snagged a Russian diver by the leg. The man writhed and twisted. McNeil fancied he could almost hear the man screaming in terror. Then the other claw reached out and gently plucked the man's mouthpiece from between his lips. For a moment his struggles were more frantic than ever; then they stopped for good.

As the third man stopped struggling, McNeil saw Nielsen dart across the viewport, living up to his nickname. With the ease of a shark overtaking a flounder Nielsen caught up with the fourth diver. The Russian turned to fight, but as he turned, Nielsen's hand came up, holding a pellet gun. Two puffs of gas, and a steel sliver drove into the Russian's chest, another into his brain. He drifted down toward the bottom, the disturbed water turning him slowly over and over like a falling leaf.

McNeil let out a long sigh of relief and wiped the sweat out of his eyes. Then he called John Cheever.

"We've—cleaned out—all four. Do you want their—torpedo—for a souvenir?"

"Well done, both of you. No, just get it out of the way. It's probably booby-trapped against tampering. I don't want to push our chances." A pause. "Are you both in shape to run another mission—right now?"

"I am—I think," said McNeil. Actually what he most wanted right now was a half hour alone, a cigarette, and a long, cold beer or maybe several. But the first two were impossible aboard the deep diver, and the third was illegal aboard any ship of the United States Navy. Apart from that, though, he was game for another round with the Russians.

Nielsen came on the line with, "Aye aye, sir."

"Good," said Cheever. "The executive officer is suiting up and coming out to join you with a—calling card—for our friend."

"Oh," said McNeil.

"Yes," said Cheever. "After all—he sent us one. It's only good manners to do the same to him."

## 22

The big desk with the sign "Administrative Assistant" was empty when Admiral Cappel arrived at Senator Bergen's office. There was no Charles Pender to greet him, either politely or impolitely. Since Charles Pender had been arrested by the FBI two hours ago, this didn't particularly surprise the admiral.

It would, however, be a surprise to Senator Bergen, unless Pender or Pender's lawyer had called up the office in the twenty minutes since Cappel had talked with David Wilton. At that time the FBI agent had assured Cappel that no word of the arrest could have reached the Senator.

Cappel hoped Wilton was right. Dropping this particular bombshell on the Senator's desk would rock him back on his heels from the start. Whatever they eventually hammered out between them, Cappel wanted to make the Senator sweat just a little if he could.

A junior secretary led Cappel into the Senator's office. The secretary was red-haired and bouncy—definitely an improvement over Pender. Senator Bergen looked exactly the same as ever. Cappel looked at him as intently as possible without being impolite, but saw no signs that anything was bothering the man.

"Good afternoon, Admiral Cappel," said Bergen. "I'm afraid I won't be able to give you much time. I have another appointment at four."

"Don't worry, Senator. What I want to say won't take much time."

"I hope you're not coming to make another plea against the investigation of your office, Admiral Cappel. I admit I spoke in haste the last time. I'm not really planning to deal with you that soon. But if you are going to insist on arousing my suspicions ..." The Senator let his voice trail off. He was obviously trying to project his "come let us reason together" image full blast. Cappel, who had known and respected the late Lyndon B. Johnson, couldn't help feeling that the late President had done it a good deal better.

"Senator Bergen," said Cappel crisply. "I think circumstances have arisen which might cause you to reconsider your investigation of the Office of Special Submarine Operations. Your administrative assistant has been working for the Russians. He was arrested about three hours ago for espionage and as an accessory to first-degree murder."

"What the hell are you talking about?" snapped Bergen. "Have you come here to make some sort of bad joke at my expense or—"

"I'm not joking, Senator," said Cappel, in a voice about the temperature of liquid hydrogen. "Charles Pender was recruited by Russian intelligence about five years ago, while he was in college. We don't have all the circumstances yet, so it may have been a case of blackmail or pressure. But the facts are indisputable." That was almost certainly being too charitable to Pender, from what David Wilton had said. It was long odds against Pender's being anything but a willing agent. But there was no need for Bergen to believe that and no point in wasting time trying to convince him.

168

Bergen's voice was more controlled this time when he spoke. "Admiral Cappel, I find it hard to believe that Charlie has even been arrested. No, on second thought—even an admiral wouldn't play jokes like this. But I seriously doubt that there is any evidence against him that will stand up in a court of law. I think you and the FBI have arranged a frameup of Charlie to discredit me. If that's the case, I'll—" The craggy face turned very red and Bergen fell silent, as if he couldn't think of anything bad enough to threaten Cappel with.

Cappel took advantage of the silence to shove a slip of paper onto the Senator's desk. "Senator Bergen, why don't you call that number before you make any more threats?"

Bergen looked at the paper, and his face burned even redder. "Why?"

"You may find it easier to believe me then, Senator. And as you yourself said—'even an admiral wouldn't play jokes like this.'"

For a moment it looked as if Senator Bergen were going to have a stroke on the spot. His breath came in short gasps, and both hands clutched hard at the arms of his chair. Then, with an obvious effort, he got himself somewhat under control and dialed the number. He had to make three tries before he got it right.

But at least his voice was steady as he spoke.

"Good afternoon, Mr. President. I've been asked to call you by an Admiral Hugh Cappel from the—oh, you know him? No, Mr. President, I wasn't— Anyway, he's described a rather nasty situation that's suddenly come up about my chief assistant, Charles Pender, and—"

That was the last word Bergen spoke for quite a while. But his hands kept clenching and unclenching faster and faster, and his face gradually went from red to its normal color. Then it kept on changing until it was very pale. When Bergen hung up the telephone, his right hand was no longer clenched. It was shaking slightly.

Cappel deliberately let the silence drag on, looking steadily at the Senator as he did so. As he had expected, it was Bergen's nerves that broke first. In a voice that was no steadier than his hands, he said, "All right. I—have to believe you. At least it—seems serious enough, if the President is— Well, never mind about that." He sighed and straightened his shoulders. "What do you want, Admiral Cappel?"

Cappel was tempted to tell the Senator that he didn't need to surrender before he was even asked. Granted that Cappel had just landed a blow from a very heavy club, the speed at which Bergen had folded was still a little disappointing. Politicians, thought Cappel. It's a game to them. When somebody changes the rules and starts playing for keeps— But there was no point in letting his mind run along those lines. It was time to lay out his case before Bergen.

"Do I need to tell you what it would mean if word got around that Pender was a subversive and a major security leak? Specifically, what it would mean to your ability to carry on the investigation of illegal intelligence operations?"

Bergen leaped at the second question like a trout at a particularly mouth-watering fly. Apparently he wasn't quite so cowed as Cappel had thought. "Then you admit illegal intelligence operations have been carried out?"

"Of course," snapped Cappel. "Not by my office— that's not our job. We're a research and development group—that's what's 'special' about us. But as for some of the other agencies—I'm an admiral, not an idiot. Of course some of the other agencies have been a bit grabby, and I see no reason not to slap their hands. I don't want to interfere with your investigation, in general."

170

Bergen was staring at Cappel as though the admiral had just offered him the key to Fort Knox. "You're serious?"

"Of course. Foreign intelligence operations are one thing. Spying on our own citizens is something else again. I'm quite sure you and I see more or less eye to eye on the second point. Maybe we even agree on the first, since we both have the interests of this country at heart. We both serve it, in different ways." It suggested how numb Bergen really was that he didn't react to the admiral's flattery.

"In any case, Senator Bergen, if you push the investigation of O.S.S.O., you'll be wasting your time and the taxpayers' money. You'll also be taking on both my office and the FBI on top of all the other enemies you're bound to make sooner or later. You'll be making it certain that the Pender affair gets spread all over the newspapers. And you won't be gaining a damned thing by any of it."

"All right, Admiral," said the Senator. "What's the alternative?"

If Bergen hadn't kept licking dry lips, he would have looked as though he were honestly seeking information—rather than the way out of a trap.

"Take O.S.S.O. off your list of agencies to investigate—at least for the time being. If you want to double-check later, we can work something out. We may even be able to arrange that tour of our facilities that you mentioned the last time I was in. Under suitable conditions, of course, but I think it might be possible.

"In return, the FBI man in charge of the Pender case and I can see that no more of it gets out than is absolutely necessary. I don't know how far we'll be able to push this—the FBI man already has his job on the line. But I think we can be pretty sure the CIA won't be able to pick it up. That will keep the one group that you and I both have to worry about off our

171

backs. You know what the CIA is like when it gets on the warpath."

Bergen managed a chuckle. "I do indeed."

"So," Cappel finished, "there's no need for any big rumpus, if you'll just let us alone for the time being. No trouble for us, no trouble for you." He paused. "Do we see eye to eye on this?"

Bergen was silent for quite a while before replying. "Admiral, I can't honestly say either yes or no just like that. It's been—rather a shock to me. Could I call you back this evening? I won't take more than a few hours, I promise you."

Cappel hesitated a moment before answering. Taking the pressure off Bergen might give him the will to fight back. But keeping the pressure on might drive him into a corner, where he would try clawing his way out like a trapped animal. Either could end up giving O.S.S.O. more trouble than if Cappel had never come to see the Senator at all.

Finally he made his decision. "All right, Senator. I'll be in my office until well after dinnertime, so you can get me there. I'll leave you with this, though." He reached into his briefcase and pulled out two large envelopes. "This one is the dossier on Charles Pender. The other is a summary of O.S.S.O.'s facilities and activities. I'd rather you didn't mention to anybody that you'd seen them, however. All right?"

Bergen nodded silently and took the envelopes. The two men shook hands; then Cappel got out of the office as fast as possible.

Outside, he couldn't help wondering if he had made the right decision. Any dealings with Bergen were a gamble. But the approach he had used was probably the best. It wasn't as emotionally satisfying as driving Bergen into a corner would have been, but it would probably work out better for O.S.S.O. and *Devilfish*.

Cappel stopped in midstride at the thought. It was a

measure of how much he had been concentrating on Bergen that he hadn't thought about *Devilfish* all day. How far had Johnny Cheever pushed his duel with the Russian submarine?

## 23

The water around them was dark. But Frank Bronson and Chief Nielsen had infrared torches to light the water and infrared goggles to look for their prey. It was possible that prey might have external sensors alerted for visual light. It was unlikely that it would be equipped to pick up infrared.

Their prey was the Russian submarine, lying on a shelf of rock just above them. Fifty feet below, bobbing like a balloon on the end of its anchor cable, was the deep diver. Doctor McNeil was still at the controls. Bronson couldn't help wondering how he could ever have doubted the scientist's courage or competence. For whatever reason, he had done it, and for that he owed Doctor McNeil an apology.

But that could wait until they were back aboard *Devilfish*. Right now there was a calling card to deliver, an ingenious and surprising one that made Frank Bronson grin every time he thought of it.

He kicked his way upward another fifteen feet and flicked the torch on, shining it into the darkness ahead of him. Just at the limits of visibility, a massive, rounded metal surface thrust out toward the two Americans.

"Good," said Bronson. He kept the light on for a few more seconds, firmly committing to memory the position and angle of the Russian submarine. Then he looked at the luminous compass dial on his right wrist and picked the course he estimated would bring them to the Russian's stern. Finally he switched off the light and motioned to Nielsen. They swam forward into the darkness.

Underwater scuba navigation in total darkness was something Frank Bronson normally took in his stride. But he had never had to play ring-around-the-rosy with a full-sized Russian submarine before. They had to reach the Russians' stern, preferably without using their lights and certainly without striking against any part of the enemy's hull. That risked alerting the Russians. If they had more divers they might send them out. If they didn't, they could at least start up their engines and flee, leaving *Devilfish* with only a small victory.

Frank Bronson wanted a full victory. So did John Cheever.

Two minutes, three, four. The closed-circuit oxygen-helium scuba outfits made no bubbles in the water. The only sound was their own breathing and occasional faint clanks and thuds carried through the water from inside the Russian ship. Bronson was able to use those sounds as a rough guide to his location. When they started fading out below him, he turned around and shone his light downward.

He had guessed correctly. Directly below lay the stern of the Russian submarine, a massive steel cone with four huge fins. At the junction of the fins the marine bronze of the six-bladed propeller had a weird sheen in the infrared light.

No need for words now. Bronson pointed and he and Nielsen drifted cautiously down until they were level with the propeller. What they were about to do they had rehearsed many times. But this was the first time against a live enemy, at least for Bronson.

Each man carried two long plastic tubes slung on his belt—four in all. They took three of the tubes and tied one around the base of each of the three portside blades of the propeller. The tubes now looked like giant doughnuts.

Bronson pulled a loop of wire sticking out from each doughnut. This ruptured a seal that kept the water out of a special adhesive compound that set like rock when exposed to sea water. Then they held each doughnut tightly in place for a few seconds to give the adhesive time to set solidly. The three doughnuts were now fastened around the three propeller blades so firmly that nothing short of an explosion could dislodge them.

Bronson was tempted to place the fourth doughnut against one of the fins, but decided against it. He couldn't be sure how much extra flooding that would produce. Perhaps enough to sink the Russian, which wasn't really the idea. So he hooked it back on his belt. Then he took three slim tubes, each about the size of a large felt-tipped pen, out of a pouch on the belt. He thrust one firmly home into each of the three doughnuts, feeling them sink down into the solid paste. Only the last inch of each one was sticking out. With his clasp knife, Bronson carefully peeled the plastic cover off each one of those ends. Then he backpedaled away from the propeller and briefly switched on his light. Everything was in place, and there was no sign the Russians had noticed anything.

He motioned to Nielsen. Without a word the two men finned upward until they were thirty feet above the unsuspecting Russian sub. Then they swam off into the darkness, heading for their rendezvous with the deep diver and the trip home to *Devilfish*, waiting four miles away.

The deep diver had barely settled into its cradle aboard *Devilfish* when the three men aboard it heard Cheever's voice in their earphones. It was the first human sound they had heard in nearly two hours.

"Welcome home, gentlemen. All set?"

"Four-oh, sir," said Bronson. "All three charges placed and armed. We set them for thirty-five knots at four hundred feet."

"Any chance they detected you?"

"A pretty small one."

"All right. That will have to do. We're going to start up the engines and get out of here as fast as possible. And—well done, all of you. See you in a few minutes." The telephone went dead. Before the three men could move, they felt the vibration of *Devilfish's* engines reaching them through the hull of the deep diver.

"Not wasting any time, is he?" said McNeil, as he reached back to open the inner hatch.

"No," said Bronson. "Why should he? Our surprise isn't going to be any good until we're going fast and deep."

"The American has started his engines," said the soundman on duty aboard *Thunderbolt*. "Slow speed only—about thirty rpm. And he appears to be blowing ballast."

That probably meant the American was getting ready to leave. And the divers not back yet! Lukin stared at the steel bulkhead in front of him as if the instruments that studded it could tell him something. But he knew they could not tell him what had happened to the divers or what he should do about it.

The divers would not be out of air yet. They had nearly ten hours' supply in their tanks and aboard the torpedo. Were they lost? Improbable, considering the precise directions they had been given. Had they met with an accident? That was always possible. But they

176

were all highly competent and well equipped. Had the American contrived to meet them and—finish them? Lukin wished he could dismiss that as impossible, but found he couldn't.

But whatever had happened to them, the divers weren't likely to return before *Thunderbolt* had to head out to sea after the Americans. That could be embarrassing. Not the probable deaths of the four divers—they were expendable. Admiral Barsukov would say little or nothing to that. But if the divers were found, dead or alive, by the British—well, it could cause trouble. The British were weak and feeble when it came to protesting as a rule, but sometimes they could nerve themselves to make a great deal of noise.

"Comrade Captain, the American submarine has appeared on the sonar. Distance seven thousand meters, bearing 330, speed ten kilometers, depth one hundred meters. He appears to be reversing—ah, no, now he's turning around. A very tight circle, Comrade Captain." A long pause. "He's heading out to sea, still at ten kilometers."

"Thank you," said Lukin. The American had made the choice for him. The divers would have to take their chances, with the British, with their air supply, with everything else. He could not simply let the American sail away into the broad Atlantic to save four divers.

He reached for the microphone. "This is the captain. All hands to station for getting underway."

John Cheever's voice came over the PA system, audible above the roar of the showers as McNeil and Bronson scrubbed off the sweat and grime of their mission. "This is the captain. We are being followed again by our old friend."

"Here we go again," said McNeil. He had used up all his adrenalin running the deep diver four solid hours, and he was finding it hard to keep interested in what was going on outside. "What happens now?"

"The captain's going to cruise north for a while, I suspect. He'll want to see if the Russian goes back to his old habit of matching us for course and speed. If he does—"

McNeil nodded. "If he does, we can more or less set—our calling card—off any time we want. Right?"

"Right."

"The American has increased speed to twenty-five kilometers," said the soundman.

"Very good," said Lukin. He ordered the engine room to match the increased speed appropriately, then leaned back in his chair. It was likely that there would be very little to do for the next few hours as they ran north from St. Helena. They would have to be alert for any sudden change of course or speed; otherwise, they might drop back beyond reliable range for detonating the limpet mines. But there would be no major decisions to make. They could let the American lead toward his fate.

An hour went by, then a second, then a third. At three hundred feet below the surface and fifteen knots, the two submarines headed north. Aboard *Devilfish* there was a strong feeling of "Haven't we done all this before?" The only difference from the week's voyage south was that the Russian submarine was staying closer now—only about six miles astern, instead of eight to ten.

Cheever was taking the con himself, sitting in the main control chair and watching the display cube with a thin smile on his face. Then the intercom went beeep.

"Control room." It was Kitter again, handling the sonar and listening gear. "I'm picking up a surface contact at about ten thousand yards. Dead ahead, heavy twin screws, about one-twenty rpm. Sounds like a merchant vessel."

All the emotion drained out of Cheever's face. His voice was completely flat and neutral as he said, "Engine room. Thirty knots."

On the other side of the control room, Frank Bronson took a deep breath. This was the moment of commitment—for John Cheever, for *Devilfish*, for everyone aboard her. And also for the Russian submarine.

For a second Bronson wondered why Cheever was picking the moment when they were approaching an unidentified merchant vessel to make his move. The answer came almost in the same thought.

If the Russian had to surface in distress, it was just as well that a ship would be there to help her. Otherwise *Devilfish* herself would have to come to the aid of her late enemy. The laws of the sea and John Cheever's iron sense of his duties under those laws would require it. Even though it might mean risking *Devilfish*'s security, he would do it, even if he received a direct order not to. But he would certainly never receive such an order from Admiral Cappel.

Bronson took another deep breath and stared at the display. The merchant vessel was appearing on it now—a white dot on the surface. But the Russian was still where it seemed he had always been.


"The American has increased speed to fifty kilometers," came from the sound room.

"Why the sudden hurry?" Lukin asked himself. Had the American captain's nerves finally broken under the strain of being constantly followed? In any case, they could not afford to lose him. St. Helena was still a little too close to permit *Thunderbolt*'s move.

"Increase speed to fifty kilometers."

*Devilfish* passed almost directly under the merchant vessel, three hundred feet down and moving at thirty knots. On the display Cheever saw that the Russian submarine had closed to five miles.

It was time.

"Thirty-five knots," he said quietly. "Take her down to six hundred feet."

Aboard *Thunderbolt* the watchers detected *Devilfish*'s increase in speed and saw her going deeper. They passed the information on to Commander Lukin, and he gave his usual orders.

As *Thunderbolt* reached thirty-five knots and passed four hundred feet, the pressure around her racing propeller reached a critical point. Three hydrostatic plungers drove inward, completing three electrical circuits. Three detonators fired. A split second later, the devastatingly powerful explosive in the three doughnuts around the three propeller blades went off.

Instantly the three blades on the port side of the propeller sheared off and were flung away into the sea, to drift down to the bottom and lie there forever. The dynamic stresses on the propeller shaft itself—five tons of steel with a ten-ton propeller rotating at two hundred and fifty rpm—became spectacularly, horribly unbalanced.

Metal screamed in protest as the propeller shaft twisted itself like taffy. The sealing glands in the shaft tunnel ruptured, letting sea water pour into the engine room. Bearings fractured or melted, sending bits of metal slicing through the air, cutting down men and cutting through wiring. Hull plates bulged, seams strained and then gaped, letting in more water.

Aboard *Thunderbolt*, pandemonium reigned.

It took Lukin barely thirty seconds to realize that he had lost his fight. It took him less than thirty more to realize that he might lose his ship as well. By the time he had given the orders to blow all ballast, the rising water in the engine room had already started short-circuiting electrical gear. By the margin of a few seconds only, Lukin acted in time.

The bridge watch of the British tramp steamer *Glennaird* watched in amazement as *Thunderbolt*'s long black hull surged up out of the sea. They continued to watch as she wallowed helpless in the heavy swell, lurching drunkenly. They only moved into action when they saw a signal lamp winking from the submarine's bridge—winking a distress signal in international Morse code.

If they had kept on watching, they might have noticed a slim periscope rise out of the sea about three miles away and five minutes later. It did not stay up long, though. Just long enough for John Cheever to snap a few color pictures, before *Devilfish* plunged down deep again.

# 24

In Washington they had to rout Admiral Cappel out of bed to give him the message from *Devilfish*. When he read it, he burst out in roars of laughter.

In Murmansk they brought the message from *Thunderbolt* to Admiral Barsukov in his office. He exploded in a terrible stream of curses and swept the chess pieces off the board with his steel-clawed left arm. Since Captain Volynsky was only two moves away from checkmating the admiral, it didn't matter anyway.

Eight hours later John Cheever, Lerone McNeil, and Frank Bronson were sitting around the wardroom table aboard *Devilfish*. Cheever was summarizing the messages that added up to an end to the crisis.

"Bergen has agreed to leave the office alone for the time being and cooperate with the FBI's investigation of Pender. That may lead them back to the people who actually got Connie Gilman."

"What about a larger appropriation for O.S.S.O.?" asked McNeil. Six hours' sleep had ironed a good many of the lines out of his heavy face and strengthened his voice.

"Don't worry about that, Doctor," said Cheever. "Cappel didn't want to ask for that directly. But with the office no longer under investigation, we've got enough friends in Congress for one of them to propose a larger appropriation. And we're likely to have enough votes to get it through."

"Good," said McNeil.

"What about our Russian friend?" said Bronson.

"*Thunderbolt*—that seems to be her name—is being towed to St. Helena for the time being until she is out of danger of sinking."

"Who's doing the towing?"

"That steamer we passed, the British *Glennaird*. The British are also sending out a frigate to escort them in, just in case some Russian 'trawler' wants to move in too close. They're going to send down a team of 'salvage experts'—from the office of the admiral commanding submarines. They'll give *Thunderbolt* a good going-over, inside and out, before they let her go. I have a feeling a few heads are going to roll in Moscow over this."

"I hope so," said Bronson enthusiastically. To Cheever's surprise, McNeil nodded.

Before Cheever could go on, Chief Steward Perez appeared, carrying a plate of fresh doughnuts and wearing a broad grin. "New hot batch, sir. Try them, please."

There was something in Perez's voice Cheever couldn't quite place. Anticipation? In any case, why pass up a good doughnut? He reached out, took one, and bit out a chunk.

"Mmmm," he said, "Interesting flavor. Did O'Hara use buckwheat flour for these?"

McNeil grinned. "O'Hara didn't make these, Captain. And the cook who made them didn't use flour. He used the latest batch from the processor."

Cheever stared at the scientist for a minute, then took another bite out of the doughnut. Yes—he could just detect a slight tang and a lumpiness that wasn't normally there. But if he hadn't been looking for it—?

"Congratulations, Doctor," he said. He took a second doughnut while Perez refilled his coffee cup.

The three men sat, silently enjoying their triumph, as Devilfish raced north.